Read #2 in the

Groundswell Sagas

'Game On'

Go to:

www.groundswellsagas.com

Enjoy!

Toby Garrard

Building 9

Toby Garrad

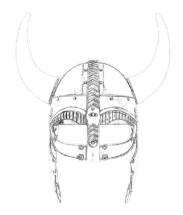

Groundswell Sagas
Book 1 (of 4)

REBEL
MAGIC
BOOKS

REBEL
MAGIC
BOOKS

To Susan, Taya & Finn

for supporting the journey turned adventure

Contents

Prologue 9

1. Kill House 11
2. Betrayal 16
3. Tough & Competent 19
4. Silver 24
5. Aftermath 29
6. Coyote 33
7. Stall 36
8. The Hub 38
9. Bio Flaw 42
10. Darkness 45
11. Zone 4 48
12. Adventdalen 52
13. Outpost 55
14. Shrund 60
15. Armageddon 64
16. Oval Ultimatum 67
17. Firing Room 72
18. Viking 74
19. NASA One 81
20. Playbook 84
21. The Pit 86
22. Melt Down 90
23. Red Jacket 93
24. Weird Science 95
25. One to warn 97
26. Tourist Trap 99
27. UNIS 104
28. Purple Flare 105
29. EISCAT 106
30. Warning Word 108
31. Abominable Snowman 109
32. Gifts 110
33. Hagglund 112

34. Exodus 115

35. Mariner 117

36. Milkround 120

37. Licorice Water 122

38. Rip and Tear 127

39. Bird 130

40. The Bin 134

41. Aqua 139

42. Red Legend 143

43. Avatar 147

44. Runflat 150

45. Highlander 153

46. Super Guppy 155

47. Outsider 159

48. Finkle 165

49. Talmine 169

50. Mellness 172

51. Badger 173

52. Eagle Tree 177

53. Bagpipes 181

54. Ellington 184

55. Triple-A 188

Epilogue 191

Acknowledgments 194

About the Author 195

Prologue

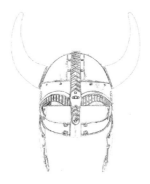

Erik the Red unleashed fire and fury from Svalbard, the land of the banished Viking. Sacking Iceland, vanquishing Greenland, he colonized Vinland—land of the vines—named by Amerigo Vespucci, claimed by Christopher Columbus, and crowned America half a millennium later.

The victorious Viking set sail for Norway in a fleet of dragonships weighed down by the treasure of conquest, but none was more valuable than the talisman—the mystical runestone by which he navigated.

Mother Nature was in no mood to ease their passage, unleashing the storm of storms, shredding sails, and shattering masts. She devoured all but Erik the Red's ship in the Labrador straights.

With the proof of conquest lost, he abandoned course and made for Bruich in Alba, the land where it all began. The last of the sea warriors stormed the former Scottish stronghold, craving the sacred place. The banished Viking knelt in the home of the runes and held the talisman aloft. Vengeance flamed in the green and gold of Erik's eyes as he pointed his sword at the heavens, demanding answers from the gods themselves.

The legend of the runestones was lost to millennia, blurred by Scottish myth and Norwegian legend. Until the girl with the green and gold eyes returned.

1 Kill House

Valhalla, Hall of the Slain, where the souls of warriors
who died nobly in battle are received.
Valhall, Odin sin hall, der sjelene til vikingar
som fell i edel kamp havner.
Norse Mythology

"This changes everything," Viking cursed, her chest heaving, the glow from her battle axe declaring their position.

"Yeah, it sucks when your rescuers are sent to kill you," Mariner replied, his face sprawled in the dirt next to hers. "Dude, look on the bright side. Death is good for the ratings."

"Call me that again, and I swear—"

"Man, y'all Norwegians have zero sense of humor." Mariner checked himself for fall damage, spitting blood on the ground.

"Repay treachery with lies," Highlander grumbled, inching his way towards their voices in the darkness, his weapon smoking. "It explains why they keep coming. There are no winners in this game. We should blow our 'friends' out of the sky, if they ever arrive."

"One last attack, one last wave. That's what we figured," Viking said. Everything they'd trained for, everything they stood for, came down to this moment, yet she'd missed it. The double-cross. One central truth—survival—surrounded by a hundred lies. There were no rules in the finale. Mariner had been right from the start; Highlander too. But

Groundswell, their environmental movement, could still succeed, even as death circled them like vultures, she convinced herself.

"Y'all Scots are only happy when you're miserable," Mariner said, looking for his wingman in the chaos of the derelict building.

"Aye, and you Americans have an answer for everything. So, make me happy by zipping it."

"Chill!" Viking demanded.

The stress of battle lurked behind her team's humor. High adrenaline masked their nerves and fatigue dulled their senses. But the playbook—their code of conduct—had got them this far and wouldn't let them down now, its thousand year old wisdom authored by Erik the Red himself.

Viking buried her axe, plunging the room into inky darkness. "Weapons, ammunition, life systems check. Now!"

"Aye, Cap. I'm on your left side," Highlander confirmed, checking his bolt-action sniper's rifle. "Fifty-cal intact. Five rounds. Life systems fifty percent. It was a hard landing."

"Dude, same. Call us twins. I took some heat covering Highlander's ass back there," Mariner scoffed before his wingman could protest. "I'm still on your right, boss."

"Gives me centerstage." Viking checked her weapons, whispered the instructions, and issued the warning. "Heavy shotgun, rocket-launcher, two shots each. Life systems, eighty percent. We'll need to rock-paper-scissors to balance energy levels. Contact imminent. Cover the windows. I've got the door. Highlander, you take the left. Weapons low and ready. Standby for the counterattack."

Three questions burned in her mind. Would their rescuers finally reveal themselves? And if so, could they help with Groundswell's insane mission? But mostly, was it all worth it?

Viking remembered to breathe. She knew that their every move, every word, every doubt was being analysed. A thousand eyes watched, millions by now. The spectators thirsted for controversy.

"Y'all hear the booming music down the street? Man, it's messing with my head," Mariner complained.

"Not your genre then? Guess it beats the cap's playlist," Highlander teased.

"What? Her hands-in-the-air rave music? It might be appropriate if this play doesn't work," Mariner winced.

Highlander's voice turned serious. "The music's a decoy. *Hud* your tongue; listen, it's stopped. They're close."

Viking rolled to her side, avoiding the smoldering launcher, rehearsing the play in her mind. "Guys, all I can hear is an American heartbeat and Scottish banter. Both of you calm it, else we're going to make a mistake. This isn't the first time we've been here, but it will be the last if you don't trust our playbook."

"Dude, that thing you shout, when you do crazy—" Mariner queried.

"Valhalla," Viking answered.

"What's it mean?"

"Hall of the Slain," Viking explained. "Where the souls of warriors who died nobly in battle are received. Norse Mythology."

"Why's it not in the playbook?"

"I don't do myth and legend," she lied. Before they'd met, all she'd done was trawl the internet searching for clues about her ancestry. "On my mark, sixty seconds. Feel the vibration in your hands. They're coming. The final fight."

Month after month, battle after battle, house to house, hand to hand, it had come down to this.

Muzzle flashes illuminated their excuse for shelter as Viking called the play. "Enemy's close range. Small arms. They're light on weaponry. Woah! Airblast! RPG!" She'd made her first mistake.

The rocket-propelled grenade obliterated the upper deck. Rafters burned, lighting the room, as embers rained down on them like fireflies.

"Called that one wrong, dude!" Mariner grimaced, staring at the stars through the ceiling.

"My bad," Viking acknowledged. "Watch those timbers. Kick out those fires," she warned, as the rest of the roof collapsed, forcing them to roll left and right.

"Down!" Mariner yelled, as heavy machine gun fire wreaked havoc through the room at waist height. "The threat's on us, man."

"Nothing like stating the obvious," Highlander said, flicking his weapon off safety.

"Guys, their triangle of fire has failed," Viking announced, seizing the initiative in the moment of silence that followed. "Three Uglies reloading. Break out now! Window, window, door!"

Viking knew it was down to muscle memory. Nothing more could save them now.

"Aye, Cap. I have visual," Highlander trained his weapon. "Two targets acquired. Ugly one at one-eighty degrees, a thousand yards out. Ugly two at two-seventy degrees, closer by half. But I *cannae* take both. Engaging Ugly one now. Snap!"

"Copy that, Highlander. Ugly two's mine." Mariner's nerves distorted his voice. "Eyeballed Ugly three. He's coming at us full frontal. Boss, you fix?"

"Copy that. Ugly three's mine," Viking confirmed, taking up position behind the door. "Guys, call your kills. Be my eyes."

"Cap, this joker's got auto-aim," Highlander warned. "I'm down to my last two rounds. I need to lure him out with a decoy shot. Steady does it. Ugly one down. I'm out of ammo!" Highlander shouted, crouching behind the remnants of the wall.

"Dude, Ugly two's shooting round corners. Sounds like a Gatling. A hundred yards out. I'm switching to semi-auto. Mariner dived to avoid the heavy machinegun peppering the bricks around them before returning fire recklessly, missing his target. He kissed his last bullet and dialed in the new range. He prepared to loose off the round, talking himself through the killing process, before squeezing the trigger from first to second stage. "Steady, breathe, psych, understand this—Ugly two neutralized. I'm out."

She knew it was now or never. All eyes were on her. A million voices were yelling *Kill* at the screen. She had one image in her brain. One thing on her mind. "Heads down, stay down!" Viking warned, bracing herself against the back wall.

"Too close," Highlander whispered urgently.

His captain removed the safety with a click, aiming the launcher at the door.

"Runa, don't!" Too late, he realized he'd named her.

Her cover blown, she snapped out of her killing trance. "That one's on you, Scott," she grumbled, making the same mistake.

2 Betrayal

One must howl with the wolves one is among.
Ein lyt tute med dei ulvar som er ute.

Their identities revealed, their call names abandoned, the teenagers entered a new world of risk. Runa knew she was exposed—they both were, due to her friend's slip-up. The GameMaster was now free to profile their private lives, along with spectators and the rest of the world.

"Plan B," Runa Erikson said, squeezing the trigger. The RPG's exhaust tail thrust her forward, the point blank blast launching her back, surprising their assailant at the instant she needed to reload. But she found herself facing the back wall, life systems wailing, frantically searching for the launcher. Her gameplay crumbled along with the building. Her fingertips found the axe as the enemy bore down, and her hand closed around its wooden shaft in the darkness. The marauder's footsteps quickened. Runa acted on instinct, hurling the ancient weapon backward toward the hole that was the door and awaited her fate.

The double-headed axe spun wildly, blade over shaft, accelerating through the air. Its razor-sharp edges sought, found, and impaled the marauder swooping in for the kill, sending its murderous intentions to the grave.

Runa got the second she needed. Her team was right, they were entering uncharted territory. It was more than a feeling; betrayal approached. But the voice in her head goaded her. The flame of vengeance flickered in the green and gold of her eyes. *"Søk noko, risiker alt."* Seek something, risk everything, she whispered, reminding herself of the gameplay she'd yet to write.

Mariner was the first to speak, hamming up his American accent. "Cover's blown now, dude. Just like the door. Y'all thinking ratings?"

"Aye, sorry for that Chase. Rats!" Scott repeated the mistake, rolling the r's of his apology in his gruff Scottish accent.

"Share the love, dude. We're all out in the open now." Chase tossed the empty rifle.

"Crackerjack play by Runa," Scott said sarcastically, pushing through the debris.

"Amen to that. The Dude didn't see it coming. Gonna dance on its grave for the ratings?" Chase asked, the American dusting himself off.

"Guys, chill. It's all about the rescue now. We need the maximum number of spectators for the sake of Groundswell." Runa picked out the launcher from the debris and disguised its broken trigger. She stood for the first time since they'd entered the kill house and checked her visual feed. Her voice laced with suspicion. "Life systems check."

Groundswell thirsted for controversy. The membership craved it. With her last breath, she'd give it to them, with or without a weapon.

"Dude, twenty percent."

"Cap, same."

"I'm also showing twenty percent after the blast damage. So our life signs are even. It means they can't extract a clear winner," Runa confirmed, breathing deeply to control her heart rate.

Scott joined his leader, flexing his hands as he looked to the artificial night sky. "Did you feel that? Thunder?"

"Rotors! Airborne rescue." Chase's voice.

"Extraction," Runa corrected him. "Guys, we stick to the plan."

"A or B?" Scott asked, already knowing the answer.

"B. Always B." Runa patted the launcher. "This makes me the negotiator. The stakes have never been higher. If we're going to do this, we need to vote.

Battle or no battle, they stuck to the Viking code laid down in their playbook. That's what made them different, and that's what made them winners.

"Hand on heart for go, head for no. After three, two, one—" The trio closed their eyes and voted for the hundredth time.

Runa took three short breaths. Swept along in the moment, she thought of her ancestors, hounded from the shores of the mainland. The pain of her childhood returned—she too carried the mark of the Viking in the green and gold of her eyes. She channeled her anger and quoted from the playbook, switching from Norwegian to English for the benefit of the blood-lusting spectators. *"Ein lyt tute med dei ulvar som er ute"*. One must howl with the wolves one is among.

"In the next life!" They repeated their pact, pledging allegiance to Groundswell with their customary three-fingered salute to the heart.

"Die well," she muttered for the ratings, gifting her friends the shotgun and two rounds. Axe in one hand, broken launcher in the other, she yelled the cry of the Viking. "Valhalla!"

"Runa, stick to the plan!" Scott shouted after her.

"Man, we're so busted. They're so onto us," Chase said, picking up the weapon of last resort and watching their friend charge into digital darkness.

3 Tough & Competent

"Houston, this is Evac One Ten. We have a problem. Over."

"We read you loud and clear One Ten. Over."

"Houston. No eyes on the prize. Repeat. Nobody to extract. It could be heavy camouflage or an invisibility play. Over."

"Copy that One Ten. Standby," Sky Symphony confirmed. She had everything to prove and everything to lose. The rookie flight director looked up at the tinted glass panel, as the heart of the agency looked down. The two silhouettes would have been invisible were it not for the aura of white light behind them. The founders of the Mission-X selection process surveyed their experiment. Their door wedged open, guaranteeing them a fast exit.

"Better not muck this up for me," she murmured, her stare returning to the array of screens encircling her team. Hand-picked, barely out of high school, yet playing a vital role in command of assets on the ground, the rookie punched the 'all stations override' button, seizing control of the communications channel, and requested their status. "Settle down people. Months of planning comes down to this moment. Let's go to work. Going around the horn—"

"Surgeon is go!"

"PAO is go!"

"Flight is go!"

"Evac One Ten is go!"

"Go all the way," Flight confirmed into her headset, snatching a look at the smoked glass as the rescue began.

Surgeon, the operations doctor, waivered over her console which was flashing amber.

PAO, the public affairs officer rocked, his brow glistening as his console changed, pulsing red.

Evac One Ten, the pilot, fifteen hundred miles away, closed his visor, bearing down on the trio.

"Surgeon. Confirm target life signs?"

"Confirming three heartbeats. Status 20%, 20%, 20%."

The flight director sighed. "No clear winner then."

"Houston. Evac One Ten is sixty seconds from the rendezvous point. Requesting orders. Over."

The rookie's eyes returned to the glass as if she knew. The whole team was in it up to their necks, swimming in risk. Mission-X's funding was in jeopardy and its future rested on her shoulders. Flight glanced up for a final time, her mentor's invisible stare burning down.

"One Ten, this is Flight. Prepare for a single evac. Prime hellfire for launch. Over."

"Houston. Confirm order. Is evac for one friendly? Over."

"Affirmative, One Ten. Rescue only the leader."

"Copy that, Houston. Over and out."

Flight hit PAO's intercom. "Confirm the number of *Snitch* spectators? We need to think of witnesses."

The *Snitch* app allowed the agency to spy on the candidates from every angle using random spectator battlefield footage. It gave Mission-X their edge, but it guaranteed the the world was watching Groundswell.

"Millions," PAO confirmed, his voice sounding faint. "It's gonna be a public relations disaster."

"Let's just hope it doesn't come back on us," Flight muttered offline.

"One Ten. Offer friendly half a million US dollars for a single evac," Flight instructed.

"Copy that, Houston. We confirm a friendly has broken cover. A single figure, standing on what's left of the second floor. Wielding an axe? Over."

All eyes were on Flight and her orders. The veneer of youth masked her cold intentions. Her career had barely started, yet her future with the agency was sinking.

The crackle from One Ten's radio broke sixty seconds of silence. "Houston. Offer made, but we have weapons lock on us! Over."

"Copy that, One Ten. Standby."

The Mission-X control room fell silent. "Gimme all ya got, PAO," Flight announced, looking directly at the public affairs guru who was feasting on his nails and turning a shade whiter, remaining mute as the command facility descended into newsroom chaos. Flight waved her hands in the air, returning her team's attention to the battle lines. "Keep the chatter down! One Ten, confirm reaction to offer."

"No reaction, Houston. Zero response. And we still have weapons lock on us. Over."

"Copy that. Standby, One Ten."

"PAO. Request to increase offer to one million US dollars. Contact Nine for authorization," Flight demanded.

PAO nervously made the call.

Nine was the force of good within the agency, a secret organization within the organization, headed by the two silhouettes. They conferred. "Flight's a hothead alright," said Professor Cornelius Allbright, the agency's chief scientist.

"The best kind," replied Huck Chambers, his deputy.

"Yet our candidate, Viking, is as cool as the icy land she comes from," the professor approached the opaque glass and stared at the cinema-sized screen.

Chambers approved the offer and checked their exit. "Let's see how this plays out."

"Building 9 authorizes one million US dollars for the rescue," PAO confirmed. "For the leader only."

Flight relayed the offer. Her voice was devoid of emotion. "One Ten. Offer friendly one million dollars, for a single evac."

"Copy that, Houston. Over."

Mission control held its collective breath.

"Houston. The friendly has made contact. It sounds like it's a kid. A girl. Over."

"Affirmative, One Ten. Confirm response to offer?" Flight sounded unsurprised.

"Negative response to offer, Houston. She's demanding a pass for three. Over."

"Drop smoke and launch flare countermeasures. Show her this is no longer a game."

"Copy that, Houston. One Ten out."

"This is ridiculous!" Flight shouted to PAO across the room, ripping off her headset, glaring at the gallery window. "I'm calling Nine direct."

Sky Symphony killed the call as the silhouettes stalled for time. "This is all going south," she murmured, ignoring her vibrating cell and the banging from behind the black glass.

"One Ten. Offer nine million dollars. Repeat. Nine million US dollars. Pass for one. Final offer. Over."

"Copy that, Houston."

Thirty long seconds passed before the air force extraction team responded. "Houston? The friendly, the girl? She hurled the axe!"

"One Ten. Drop hellfire. Bug out. Finish this now!"

"Copy that, Houston. Dropping hellfire."

The blast wave of silence overwhelmed Mission-X's control suite, shattered seconds later by the pilot. "Houston. The last thing the girl yelled was *Valhalla?*"

Sky Symphony slumped into her seat as the pilot's voice disappeared, his words still reverberating around the room. Her controllers looked towards their screens blankly. "This doesn't end here. Hope I never have to meet her," she murmured, looking towards the smoked glass, closing the file marked Viking. The whirr of the air-conditioning replaced the sound of radio static as the command center drowned in white noise.

The men behind NASA turned to face each other. The professor spoke in a low and calculated tone. "That was our unbreakable team," he pointed at the darkened screens. "Of tough, competent, teenagers."

"I just hope hijacking the world's most popular game to find them was worth it," Chambers replied, redialing Sky's cell. "I have a job in mind for our rising star, the rookie."

His call was interrupted by the alarm swamping the room in sound and blue flashing light. Heads rose on both sides of the glass as the computerized voice rang out. "Cover broken, evacuate Mars mission control center immediately."

"We're busted!" Chambers said.

"We always were," the professor said.

4 Silver

To be without silver is better than to be without honor.
Betre pengelaus enn ærelaus.

Svalbard. Land of the Banished Viking. Home to the descendants of Erik the Red and Lucky Leif Erikson.

Runa Erikson engaged the emergency power in KHO observatory manually and was back online—a task she'd learned four years before at the tender age of ten. You grow up fast living at the end of the world. The outage, and the storms that were responsible for it, were daily occurrences in midwinter Spitzbergen, the largest in Svalbard's archipelago of small frozen islands. It was a remote, mysterious, and extreme land, forged by ice, wind, and sea, five hundred miles from the North Pole.

She sat in the observatory's radio room, gluten-free taco in one hand, caffeine-free coffee in the other, and commanded the virtual assistant, "Call Groundswell."

"Connecting you now, please wait," responded the smooth electronic female voice. Runa used the delay to check the environmental monitors. Internal temperature +19C. External -38C. Wind speed 70mph, forecast 140mph by 9pm. Sunrise: none. Sunset: none. Three solid months of polar blackness tricked day into night, returning all but the hardiest of souls to wherever they called home. She glanced at the station clock—just enough time for the detour and to arrive at her destination, the Ark.

The Global Seed Vault, or the Ark as the Norwegians called it, was tunneled deep into the Plata Berget mountain. It concealed the most valuable room on Earth—the world's food source, protecting every seed, for every crop, from every country on the planet.

Runa's thoughts were interrupted by the grinning faces of Scott McMurdo and Chase Hudson flickering on the comms screens.

"Gaming is good!" The trio of fourteen year olds chorused the catchphrase, pledging allegiance to Groundswell, their environmental movement, with the customary three-fingered salute to the heart.

"*Betre pengelaus enn ærelaus.* To be without silver is better than to be without honor," announced the leader, her face expressionless as she quoted the wisdom enshrined in their playbook—the Viking code, their code. Runa stared at the two faces on the display. Counting them, her parenting tribe, and the chained beast outside, made for only six souls on the planet that she trusted.

It had been three hours since the teenagers had bombed out of Season 9, the world's most popular game, leaving both players and organizers wondering if the risks were worth it.

"What happened to plan B, Runa?" Scott McMurdo asked. "We'd agreed to down any chopper with the launcher."

Not going for plan B ensured Groundswell were ethical winners, and nobody needed to know that Runa's launcher didn't work.

Scott's question was interrupted by machine gun laughter.

"Dude, outstanding! Like I thought they'd change the level and skins, but man, the game's gone," Chase Hudson said in his most convincing Californian accent, leaning as far back as the chair would allow.

"Chase, you can drop the surfer slang," Runa said ruefully. "And no, I won't call you Mariner, before you ask. We don't have a million *Snitch* spectators hanging on your every word anymore. For an east coaster you crack me up."

Scott moved closer to the camera, preparing to ask again. Runa anticipated his move, disarming him with an attempt at humor. "You too *Highlander*! Any more of that *Aye Aye Cap* Star Trek nonsense and I'll beam you up."

"Two million spectators," Chase heckled, pointing to the app, watching Scott grin and back down.

"The numbers doubled in the space of fifteen minutes. Groundswell's membership trebled and is still growing. How could you not check the stats, Runa?"

"A power outage. I'm just back online, guys. We were fortunate it didn't happen mid-play."

"The joys of Svalbard and Spitzbergen. The most northerly inhabited place on earth. Right, Runa?" Living in the Scottish Highlands, Scott was familiar with the curse of no-signal.

"GameMaster sure offered a lot of loot," Chase sighed theatrically, making the V for victory sign at the camera. "When the team works, the dream works," he added, quoting Season 9's new motto.

He was referring to the largest gaming corporation on the planet, creators of the most successful team game ever. At what point the software was highjacked, and by whom, was unclear, until NASA changed GameMaster's motto to theirs, and Runa Erikson noticed.

"We agreed that plan A—take the money—was never going to work," Runa said.

"And for some unknown reason, we didn't go for plan B either?" Scott said sarcastically. "Guess we lost our silver but boosted Groundswell's ratings," he conceded.

Chase waved his copy of the playbook at the camera until he had Runa's full attention. "'I don't do myth and legend?' You're kidding me. You live and breathe the stuff. 'The ground will shake and tyrants tremble—'"

"'—when free men take up the sword," Scott completed his favorite call to action, swearing the wisdom was stolen from his countrymen.

"What would three fourteen year olds do with nine million dollars anyway?" Chase grumbled, forgetting to mute.

"You live on the high seas," Scott teased his friend. "I'm thinking surfboards, sunscreen, gills?"

"It wasn't GameMaster. It was bigger. Much bigger." Runa countered, ignoring their banter. She reached for the charm around her neck, a talisman bearing the ancient mark of the Viking, and rubbed it between her forefinger and thumb. "Guys, we had our plan and we stuck to it. Months of work. Countless battles. Same outcome every time. Except for today. They broke cover. They tried to negotiate. We've lit the fuse. Let's see who comes to put it out."

Runa held back on her hunch that NASA was behind the game; her Viking wisdom demanded it. *Det éin veit, er utrygt hos to. Det tre veit om, veit alle.* Safe to tell a secret to one, risky to tell it to two, to tell it to three is thoughtless folly, as everyone else will know.

"Dude, they weren't the only ones blowing their cover," Chase reminded Scott.

"I still don't understand why we didn't blow them out of the sky?" Scott asked, sounding defensive and flushing pink.

It was Runa's turn to look away from the camera. She broke the rocket launcher and should have told them, but the weapon made her the negotiator. Could she have trusted two friends she'd never met to ditch Plan A and reject the prize money? She'd never know, but Groundswell was also theirs, yet she kept secrets. She knew it and sensed they did too.

"The axe was more of a statement. It worked, didn't it?"

Chase returned to the stats. "Plan C certainly made you the world's youngest superhero." He waved Groundswell's app.

"Yeah, for all the wrong reasons," she retorted. Their mission was to grow and empower their environmental movement. Not to make her into some axe-wielding warrior queen, she thought.

KHO's Ultra High Frequency radio crackled into life, the voice metallic and distorted by static.

"Got to go, guys. Duty calls."

Chase whistled before hollering, "The Viking Code in the playbook. I'll crack it, Runa. Get to the bottom of your ancestry. Make it all go away," he said, enjoying the drama in his voice.

"Nothing to crack, Chase," Runa replied a little too quickly.

"He will one day," Scott said, his grin widening.

He meant her nightmare. She knew he was only trying to help. She'd searched the internet for weeks, months, years in vain. Her obsession: to dismiss her ancestry and end the hurt, stop the bullying. It had cost her mother her job on the mainland. The deeper she dug, the worse it got. The visions lay in wait each night, lurking behind her eyelids.

5 Aftermath

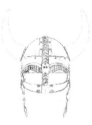

When the Team Works the Dream Works.
Når gjengen arbeider saman vert draumen oppfylt.
NASA's motto

NASA's Johnson Space Center, referred to as Space City by its devoted employees, was as integral to the human space flight program as the sun is to the universe. It was also home to Building 9, a windowless giant, where echoes have echoes. The six hundred long by one hundred foot high structure—the beating heart of the campus—was orbited by hundreds of government buildings, referred to by number only. The single-story behemoth guarded two treasures. The first, on show, was a generation of full-size spacecraft. The second—secret—was hidden deep within its foundation.

A thousand yards away, the exodus from Mission Control Building 30 was neither orderly nor unnecessary. Over four levels, it housed three mission control centers and fifty years of space flight professionalism, with one notable exception between 11.30am and 12.00pm that day. Mars Mission control on the top floor, still under construction, its rows of hybrid consoles, retina screens, and computing arrays used for months by Huck Chambers' Mission-X division, lay abandoned. The Head of NASA's human space flight program was neither alone nor innocent of hijacking the room, or The Game. He had less than five minutes to evacuate his team and get from Building 30 to the safety of Building 9, before NASA's Director One caught them.

Huck shouted over his shoulder to his chief programming intern. "Sing. Call the twins. Get one to meet us at the back entrance of Building 30 with transport, the other to fast track us through Building 9 security. Ask Darcy on reception to hold the elevator. Tell her I have the professor. And get her to stall Director One when he arrives.

To commandeer the Mars suite for Mission-X selection was risky. To dupe the US Military's Space Command to fly virtual rescue missions from Cape Canaveral was the reason they'd been caught. To offer nine million dollars of taxpayer money to a bunch of teenagers gave Director One, NASA's notorious bureaucrat, as many reasons to end Huck's career. But Chambers was passionate about everything he did, and everything he did was for NASA.

Lights flashed and warnings sounded as the thirty Mission-X gamers burst into level three's sacred Apollo mission control. The room oozed with moon landing memories, the evacuees blind to its historical importance as they stampeded toward the nearest fire escape. The curator's presentation already ruined, his guests dodged the hordes of skinny lattes racing through the national historic landmark.

Huck turned again to Sing. "Get hold of your ex-colleagues at *GameMaster*. Do not admit to hijacking Season 9, return full control immediately, blame Ransomware. We need to disguise NASA's involvement. While you're at it, tell them to change the season skins, and revert the Game's motto to theirs."

To use NASA's motto *When the Team works, the Dream works* had been both dangerous and arrogant, and had not gone unnoticed by Runa Erikson.

"But most of all, get 'em to tighten their security!"

Now it was the turn of level two to be invaded—the ISS International Space Station mission control suite, formerly Space Shuttle Command, its walls adorned by a hundred trophy plaques recognizing missions flown from within the iconic room. The nerve center was humming with intellect and concentration. Plaque STS 100 crashed to the ground as the fire doors burst open to reveal five lost gamers led by the rookie flight director herself.

Sky Symphony needed to remain anonymous. So stumbling onto the floor of the ISS mission control room a week away from her first day and offering the trio the multi-million dollar prize without her mentor's permission hadn't been the smartest move she'd made that morning. But if she found Chambers in the exodus, she planned to ask for his forgiveness.

"You're early," remarked the ISS flight controller of thirty years.

"A full week," the rookie replied to her superior.

The ISS operations team ignored the commotion. The controller continued with the emergency, purging the ammonia gas into space and the gamers back into the stairwell. Sky hid behind the collar of her leather jacket, spying Huck rushing down the fire escape.

"No doubt the professor's behind this!" The controller shouted after her.

She feigned a bow and rejoined the rabble.

"All non-essential personnel out now!" the controller announced, glad to be rid of the reporters in the gallery.

The press core followed the fleeing gamers, looking for a back story and someone to blame. Entering the emergency stairwell, they found them, their feet pounding down steel steps as they yelled at moms, listened to attorneys, and ordered Ubers.

Huck, sprinting, slammed through the ground floor fire doors, a lifetime of exercise disguising any trace of physical effort. The second of his three interns, Fox Washington, readied their transport, the mechanical ace waiting impatiently at the rendezvous point. One conspirator became three. "Where's the professor?" Fox asked in disbelief.

Sing shrugged on his cell as he listened to Fox's twin, Pearl Washington, the third intern and social media guru busy smoothing their fast-track entry to the depths of Building 9.

"Moon watches!" Huck exclaimed as he raced back toward the building. "He'll be reminiscing at the Omega wall of fame."

The professor stood spellbound, staring at the forgotten display case in the deserted tourist tunnel behind Building 30. Its shelves showcased the rows of iconic Omega timepieces. "Mercury, Gemini, Apollo, Skylab, Shuttle," he murmured, remembering each campaign fondly.

The priceless watches detailed a generation of space exploration. Gifted to astronauts, entrusted to NASA, they represented the genesis of cosmic adventure and human determination. To the professor, they defined his career of fifty years of devotion to the agency. And if it were the last time he'd gaze at them as NASA's chief scientist, he'd savor every second.

Huck tapped gently on the bulletproof glass as the distant siren wailed. "Professor, it's time to go," he mouthed. "Now!"

6 Coyote

NASA's chief scientist, Professor Cornelius Allbright, cycled like he thought. Chaotically.

Referred to by all as *the professor*, his age was uncertain, although he'd returned from retirement twice. At six foot six, his knees brushed the handlebars of the 1960s Schwinn bicycle, two hundred of which formed the principal mode of transport around Space City. The front tire wheelied, struggling to contact the ground due to the dead weight of Huck Chamber's riding on the back. The professor's grey ponytail struggled to keep up with his equally long beard, as the fugitives careered towards Building 9.

Allbright's mind was already back in the laboratory, planning how to secure his team of tough, competent, teens, his body merely a vehicle needing to catch up.

Only five hundred yards separated Building 30 from Building 9. It was a sweaty hike in Houston's summer, but a glorious stroll under a cloudless November sky, unless pursued by Building 1's director of everything, Wade Carrera, supported by a detail from Building 110 security.

"Time for a shortcut, my boy," the professor announced, mounting the sidewalk amidst a shower of coffee and donuts while scientists dived for cover.

"If it was anyone else on the planet," grumbled NASA's head of space nutrition, mourning the loss of his espresso. His not so respectful colleagues gestured their displeasure, picking the grass off their guilty pleasures as the interns followed in their bosses' wake. The professor was already engaged in his next conflict.

Space City celebrated its heritage as a nature reserve. Spread over seventeen hundred acres, it was home to over three hundred Whitetail deer. Like the free range *Schwinn* bicycles, they were owned by nobody and respected by all, save one.

Four things happened in quick succession. The professor hurtled around the final corner. Huck Chambers misjudged the severity of the turn and was sent flying with his papers into the long grass. The slumbering Whitetails scattered as if set upon by a coyote, hoofing it in one direction. And the East West doors to Building 11 opened, presenting the shortest route for the deer to the orchards behind.

Running at thirty miles an hour and jumping ten feet high, the herd chose NASA's main cafeteria as their refuge, sending its diners fleeing for their lives.

"There's only one person capable of such destruction," uttered the canteen director, hiding behind the taco stands.

"No time to be lying around sunning yourself, "the professor said unsympathetically, parking his Schwinn lovingly in the bike rack. "There is much work to be done before Director One and his security goons from Building 110 arrive."

The director of human space flight was seeing more stars than usual as Pearl dashed to his aid from the rear of Building 9. Joined by Fox and Sing, all three interns exchanged glances as they recovered the confidential paperwork marked *Accelerated Evolution*.

110 security arrived outside Building 9's front entrance leaving long tire marks on the sunbaked tarmac. Director One exited the patrol car at speed, the act of braking heard from the back entrance and the sound of the siren campus wide.

"Quick as you can, Level 9." The professor urged, as he skipped the retina scan, nodded courteously to Darcy, the Wisewoman, left guarding the elevator.

The Wisewoman had worked for Allbright since the beginning. Her heritage traced back to Rice University, the organization that sold the plot of land to NASA, creating JSC's Space City in 1965. Her real name, Darcy, no secret, but rarely used. Notorious for being the Professor's gatekeeper, it was her wisdom that defined her, sending fear down the spine of all those seeking access to the great man without good reason.

"Hold the lift," Darcy requested. "Where's Sky Symphony?"

"Gone dark," Huck replied winking. "I'm keeping my powder dry with that one. We need to keep her out of whatever happens next."

7 Stall

Director One and his security detail approached Building 9 from its east side, having found the front entrance chained. Their frustration grew as they squeezed in single file through the tiny Judas hatch fitted within the giant shuttle bay doors. Hordes of paper-waving hampered their progress, Huck's signature-seeking administrators lying in wait.

"Later, later, later!" Director One yelled, scolding them like puppy dogs. The career-obsessed ex-airforce pilot, a product of West Point, decorated for services behind a desk, was in no mood for games.

His goons muscled their way towards Building 9's elevator, forming a defensive ring around Wade Carrera. His mission was to access NASA's top secret subterranean testing complex and infiltrate Professor Allbright's private residence.

The detail, blind to the asteroid catchers, ignorant of the Martian rovers, immune to the racks of Valeri robots, homed in on the target. Their progress was halted in front of a desk staffed by a cheerful lady of senior years. The Wisewoman folded her arms, dwarfed by a backdrop of two spaceships flanking her and the elevator like colossal doormen. The size of a football field, the International Space Station loomed on her left, a full-scale shuttle simulator on her right. There was no mistaking the importance of the spot, or the woman.

Darcy smiled coldly at the VIP's security detail. "Inside voices, gentlemen. Let's start again, shall we," she said, adopting her goodbye look, waiting for silence. "How are you all doing today? State the purpose of your visit."

Director One pushed through his men, glaring at the receptionist. "Lady, it's 11.59am, technically still morning, a bad one, likely the worst in history for your boss. You know perfectly well who I am. What you don't know is why I'm here. Something so far above your pay grade it makes the real ISS look close."

The Wisewoman looked Director One in the eye, fearing nothing mortal. "If you don't adopt a civil tone with me, young man, you've got more chance of landing on the moon today," she said, buying the minutes the professor needed, delaying the security detail until 12.00pm—her mission.

Wade Carrera fumed at the woman's defiance. He clenched his fists and composed his next threat, anticipating her counterattack. He took a step forward. His jaw opened to deliver his final demand as the minute hand of the antique clock behind her chimed midday.

"One at a time," the Wisewoman said, motioning Carrera to the retina scanner with a flick of her wrist. "Have a nice—" the elevator doors clipped her words as she separated him from his men.

8 The Hub

Building 9 was as deep as it was high, disguising a complex descending nine levels to the Hub.

NASA's chief scientist believed in sacrificing sleep for success, and landing folks on the moon in the 1960s had meant sleep deprivation for a decade. The Hub became both Allbright's laboratory and home, destined to stay that way as his workload and appetite for human space flight remained unchanged. Collectively known as the Underworld, the subterranean facility was off limits to all but Allbright's closest allies, the man himself rarely leaving but for his love of super hot Lava latte.

The professor slumped into his favorite leather reading chair, its arms worn bare from years of contemplation. Comforted by the sound of his experiments as they bubbled and hissed, he smiled wryly at his predicament. Gazing into the firepit's dancing flames, he reflected on his most audacious theory to date, Accelerated Evolution. Convinced this experiment would be the one to eclipse all others, he chuckled at its codename, *Project Bones*. Like most breakthrough theories, it was beautifully simple but hugely risky.

The telltale change in air pressure derailed the professor's thought train. Huck noticed it too, his eyes locked on the elevator, watching the indicator descend slower than usual. He glanced left and right before standing. Cornelius Allbright was supremely calm. The three interns chattered nervously.

The antique ping warned of the whoosh of escaping air marking the arrival of Director One. Unsmiling, he stood alone, his security detail marooned in reception, having failed the retina scan.

The bull faced the matador—one composed and the other seething, nostrils flared, hooves raking the arena floor. It was the agonizing moment before the death charge, and Director One was at the pause. With the mind of a pilot, he considered his next move tactically, fighting the urge to rage forward and grab either man by the lapels.

Professor Allbright was NASA. He epitomized the agency—the very definition of what made it legendary—and Carrera knew he had to be careful to avoid a mutiny. The same could not be said for the director of human space flight, Huck Chambers.

Director One stepped into the professor's domain. It was his first time in the hub, despite three years running the agency. The smell hit—faint traces of cordite and gunpowder—familiar from his days in the air force. Then there was the noise. Sound from movement in all directions, winding, cranking, whirring. Carrera sensed an ambush in the dimly lit room. He rubbed his eyes as the steam rolled across the ceiling, billowing like an angry cloud, sparking red, yellow, and blue. He covered his mouth against the dry ice vapor that oozed from the ground, feeding the storm above.

"Enough of your pathetic distractions!" Carrera hollered, approaching the two men as the flames rose inexplicably from the fire pit. He folded his arms, the veins in his neck bulging. "So, our final confrontation is to be in this circus. Fitting. Your actions have created an international incident involving three sovereign countries. You've triggered a US Air Force Space Command investigation and abused NASA property. Prepare to clear your desks and kiss goodbye to your pensions. I haven't even started on the state, federal, and international legal implications."

When they didn't answer, his face flushed scarlet. "Explain!" Carrera demanded.

Huck hadn't blinked throughout the tirade. His voice harbored more than a whiff of contempt when he spoke. "We did what we had to do to locate our unbreakable team. Sir. We're now in a position to prove Accelerated Evolution."

Wade Carrera glared at the professor, who ignored him and sat staring into the flames. "Accelerated Evolution is nothing more than a mythical, unproven dream. A ludicrous quest consuming an old man throughout his entire career."

Director One resumed his attack on Huck, having received no reaction from the professor. "Chambers!" Carrera momentarily lost his composure, spit flying from his mouth. "I've sanctioned your Mission-X scam without knowing the full facts. Insane. Sponsoring the diversion of NASA resources and capital towards your selection and preconditioning program. Madness. The contempt your division has shown to offer anybody, let alone three kids, nine million dollars of taxpayer money to win Season 9, an absurd game. Inexcusable. Worse still, the whole debacle was witnessed by millions online and involved the US Air Force."

For anyone listening to the outburst, there was little doubt that the fallout would jeopardize even Director One's career.

Carrera returned to the professor, like a tiger circling its prey, his voice brimming with venom. "Your antics could not have been worse-timed. The cross-party political climate has changed irreversibly towards satellite defense systems. Human space exploration is officially a luxury. Monday's presidential insight committee will scrutinize NASA's budget, and force us to make wide-reaching cuts. You two have single-handedly signed over our budget to Air Force Strike Command!"

The professor continued staring hypnotically into the fire without a flicker of emotion.

Carrera paced in the opposite direction, shaking his fist at Huck. "You and your department have collaborated with him to willfully and deliberately mislead my organization. No more! I'm issuing you with an immediate cease and desist order for both Accelerated Evolution and Mission-X."

Carrera dismissed a nervous giggle from the interns as he surveyed the strangest room he'd ever seen. His glare returned to study the faces of the accused for any sign of acknowledgment or remorse. Receiving neither, he straightened his tie. "You have brought this on yourselves, and for what? The amusement of teenagers?"

"Fourteen year olds, to be exact," the professor said, tearing his gaze from the firepit, addressing Carrera for the first time. "As the director of human space flight has already said, Mission-X has identified the unbreakable team. Bonded by a common purpose, motivated by friendship and a fundamental belief in each other, their loyalty was tested to destruction in the Game. Surely, I need not lecture you in NASA's motto: When the team works, the dream works. It must survive to bridge another generation. The difference being the dream of Accelerated Evolution is now a reality." The flames lit Allbright's face as he stared through Carrera.

Director One backed into the elevator, reluctant to break his glare on the accused. A cruel smile transformed his face. "Wild words from a desperate old man clinging to a fantasy. Congressional insight committee in seventy-two hours. Leave no trace of your Project Bones or Mission-X. They never existed. The carnival ends here. Disband your teams. And one more thing, Allbright. Put the fire—" The antique doors cut him off, whisking him back to his career.

9 Bio Flaw

To be tough and competent. The price of admission to NASA's ranks. From that day, it got a whole lot harder.

Huck reflected on the crushing conversation with Director One as he ascended to level two in the underworld. His contempt for the man rose faster than the elevator delivering him to the home of Mission-X and his Department of Astronaut Selection and Preconditioning.

He poured an Arabian strength coffee, silenced his virtual assistant, and dropped into his swivel chair, stealing the moment he needed before the digital world devoured him.

He lashed out at the trash can from his seat, spinning full circle to face the screen. The whoosh of incoming mail interrupted his darkening thoughts, luring his eyes to the message. NASA's email filter flagged it as suspicious, warning 'potentially harmful content' and 'recommended not to trust external sources with attachments.' Huck straightened his back, all too familiar with the sender and his paymaster. He hovered the cursor over the message sent by the second most powerful organization on the planet, issued by the man who ran it, Dr Woe, the Director-General of the World Health Organization. WHO, a specialized agency of the United Nations focused on international public health. Established in 1948, it was headquartered in Geneva, Switzerland, and their emails stopped time.

Titled *Global Press Release 29th November,* Dr Woe's work bore the name *Human Physiology Deep Space Crisis Report.* Seconds later, the same title appeared in his social media account, re-tweeted.

Escalating from media shower to meteor storm, it began.

Chambers checked his watch; it was only 12.30pm. He'd already witnessed the disintegration of his cherished Mission-X program. What more could there be to lose?

His face transformed into bewilderment as the tweets fell like acid rain. *For the immediate attention of the Global Scientific Community. Author Dr Woe PhD.*

He skipped to Woe's executive summary. *Human Space Travel is biologically flawed, lethal, and from this day forward illegal.*

Huck exhaled coffee simultaneously through his mouth and nose, but at no time did his eyes leave the list of damming accusations ending the future of NASA's crewed spaceflight.

Human Physiology Crisis Report Section Summary 9.1.1. Bone Density Deterioration in Zero & Reduced Gravity: Status, Lethal. International Space Station studies unilaterally proved humanoid bones degraded at 2% per month in zero gravity. In reduced Mars gravity of 38%, bone deterioration projected at 1% per month. Anticipated astronaut bone deterioration during a standard return mission to Mars estimated at 50%, comprising of two hundred and sixty million miles, twelve months in transit, twenty-four months on a planetary surface. Casualty damage defined as permanent and irreversible.

Dr Woe's findings worsened as Huck read on.

Section 9.1.2. Pulmonary heart deterioration. Status, Serious,

Section 9.1.3. Optical deterioration in reduced gravity. Status, Dangerous

Section 9.1.4. Solar radiation exposure. Status, Critical.

As Huck reached Woe's conclusions, his heart sank with the future of his beloved agency. The NASA company man struggled to see how the professor, his oldest friend, could realize his life's work.

All fifty-one member states were to revoke funding immediately for human deep space exploration, on the basis that *such endeavors are biologically flawed and incompatible with human ethics.*

Every line on his desk flashed. The ex-director of human space flight watched his cell vibrate across the table in slow motion. Only after it clattered into the dented trashcan did he loosen his collar, spin in his seat, and march towards the elevator.

Of the 15,000 personnel working in Space City that day, 14,996 were coming to terms with the same damming information and shared a similar sense of dread. The future of NASA's human space program was in mortal danger.

Of the remaining four, three oblivious astronauts parachuted into the storm unfolding below, leaving one subterranean soul sitting in his favorite armchair, massaging his brow, warming his toes against the fire pit. NASA's chief scientist watched the elevator descend from level two, and waited for the ping.

"They need us now, my boy. More so than ever," the professor said, offering Huck Chambers a wry smile.

10 Darkness

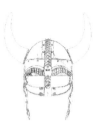

KHO, or Kjell Henriksen Observatory by its full name, was home to both Runa and her mother, but mostly Runa. Fraya Erikson, a free-spirited PhD planetary scientist, spent most of her time either measuring the Aurora Borealis or tracking space debris at the remote EISCAT radar station.

The facilities were separated by a glacial crevasse, the women by an emotional void. Their relationship was as complex as the commute, and navigation was made worse by winter's perpetual darkness and a mother's foolish pride.

Weather locked and isolated them for days—usually weeks—and the radar station was both Fraya's prison and her playground. She loved her daughter, but since the disappearance of Runa's father and the misadventure on the mainland forcing their return to Svalbard, she'd become a disciple to her work for ESA, the European Space Agency. She now shared the responsibility of motherhood with Saskia Galin, her best and only friend.

Runa reached for KHO's UHF radio as it crackled, the voice unintelligible. The trusted system required etiquette and patience, but it had its enemies, weather and eavesdroppers the worst at twelve degrees north of the Arctic Circle. The life-critical tech had no sense of humor, especially if dealing with the office of the governor, her mother, or the mainland.

The Norwegian mainland. The mere thought of the place sent a chill down Runa's spine. She'd been set upon the moment they'd arrived from the frozen north, bullied for carrying the mark of the Viking—her strange and alluring eyes. In the land where kids were suckled on myth and legend, lore made it true. They fled, hounded by their enemies, returning to Svalbard, like her ancestors a thousand years before.

The radio barked again, this time louder.

Runa waited for the warbling signal to stabilize. Her thoughts returned to the mainland. That's where it started. That's where it all went wrong, she thought. The last thing she needed was the nightmare haunting her during the day. She swallowed, punched her pack and reached for the receiver, her conscience retaliating at the sound of her mother's voice. It was all my fault. Everything, she cursed, battling the guilt to the far corners of her mind, banishing it to a land where darkness reigned supreme.

"I read you EISCAT, this is KHO Base. Over." Runa responded, a hint of weakness in her voice disguised by static. She remembered Saskia's well meaning advice for her mother: *short visits, no meals, keep the communication to as few words as possible, and just listen*!

Fraya greeted her daughter in the customary Norwegian way—practical, unemotional, cutting straight to the point. "*God morgen*, Runa. *Er du ok? Noen storm skader?*" Are you okay, was there storm damage?

"Mother, you promised. It's Friday. We practice English. I'm fine. Only light damage to the observatory. A bent transmitter on the mast. We're currently on back-up power. And before you ask, I'll do a quick perimeter check before I leave for the Ark."

Every time they left the habitat, they were in danger.

Fraya Erikson's breathless monologue began. "*Bra, forsiktig—* good, be careful, use the weather window. Do not miss your studies with Saskia at the Ark, and radio ahead to make sure everything is in order. I'll be listening, and call me upon arrival. Respect your turnaround time. No exceptions! A weather bomb's coming. Barometric readings are off the scale, so don't take any chances. And leave early. Remember to return the station power to mains before you leave, else you'll burn out the back-up generator. And you know what that means!"

Runa swallowed hard at the veiled threat of the boarding house at sea level. No way did she want to live there with the other workers' kids. It would be a setback for Groundswell and a disaster for her.

"I can see the lights of Longyearbyen, so that means the grid will be on soon. Don't forget to feed the dogs, all of them. And Runa—take the rifle, not the American's gadget. Remember what happened when you got caught with it last time. You're on your final warning with the governor!"

"But *Chirp's* the best bear-scare tech out there."

"Runa, the rifle, not *Chirp*! Over and Out."

11 Zone 4

One to warn, One to wound, One to kill.
Ein for å åtvare, ein for å såre, ein for å drepe.
Svalbard Wisdom

Svalbard, home to the King of the Arctic—the polar bear. Permanent population, 3,000. Permanent human population, 2,000.

"ARK, this is KHO Base, comms check. Over." Runa tested the radio before venturing outside. Item number two on the survival checklist after 'obey weather forecast.'

"KHO, this is ARK. I hear you loud and clear, my Runa. Over." Saskia's Russian accent was unmistakable; fierce, protective, and proud, but her questions lay in wait like the dangers of the plateau.

"Hi hi, Saskia. Expected time of arrival at ARK 3.30pm. Over."

"Repeat Runa, I lost you in the static."

"ETA 1530 hrs. I have a special delivery for the Outpost en route. Over." Runa could tell by the delay in Saskia's response that she wasn't happy.

"Respect your turnaround time, don't risk using that *Chirp* gadget, and take the rifle. Like your Mama told you!"

"Roger that. Over and out."

Saskia waited a full sixty seconds, knowing the Outpost was listening. "Attention, lazy Cossacks! You know who this is. Get mail yourselves next time. Anything happens to my Runa in zone three, I'll rip your throats out and feed your liver to the bears. *Da?*"

After a few seconds, the anonymous *"Da,"* confirmed receipt of the warning.

Svalbard was split into four zones. Only zone one, encircling the town of Longyearbyen, was designated safe. Zone two required a rifle, zone three was feared by the Vikings, and even the bears avoided zone four.

Check now or die later, Runa reminded herself. The next five minutes were critical. The first half of the list was easy, performed in the luxury of the habitat's +19C. The second was more challenging, the last chance to zip up in the comfort of the porch's +0C. And then there was outside.

She worked in a khaki T-shirt, her survival suit tied around her waist, and attacked the list with gusto. Her statuesque build, broad sporting shoulders and defined arms were the product of Viking DNA and more than a match for any boy her age. She pleated her long blonde hair in the style of a halo, declaring her striking Scandinavian features—high cheekbones, sleek jawline—to be beautiful yet understated. Her eyes told the stories of old—one as green as the amethyst she wore around her neck, the other as yellow as Inca gold.

She caught her image in the polished aluminum of the habitat and looked away, hating her reflection. It was her fault. Runa scolded herself as the guilt eked through her armor. She was the cause. She was the reason they'd been banished from the mainland.

"Sucks being different," she murmured, rechecking the inventory aloud, a habit of extreme isolation. "GPS, check. Emergency pack, check. Bodycam, check."

She circled her arms uncomfortably in the harness. Vlogging had become essential. Flashes of life at the Pole boosted ratings. While the footage was unexciting to her, it was addictive for Groundswell's followers, especially the journeys into the high-risk zones.

"Weapons, flares, rifle, ammunition three rounds." Runa hummed the Arctic nursery rhyme she'd learned as a child. *Ein for å åtvare, ein for å såre, ein for å drepe.* One to warn, one to wound, one to kill. She inspected her weapon of choice, Chase Hudson's *Chirp*—in her mind the world's best scarecrow technology, adapted for the King of the Arctic. She turned to the package for the Outpost. Finally, the chance to make the drop in zone three.

Since she'd hidden *Chirp* around Longyearbyen's outer limits, sightings of scavenging polar bears in safe zone one were rare. The same was not true for zone two, where the great beasts would still risk the guns of the tourist police. Zone three was their domain.

Runa cursed global warming for the lack of sea ice and seals, the bears' natural food source. It wasn't their fault they had to stray and forage the eco dumps for scraps. She grabbed the exposure jacket, beat the button, and braced herself for what lurked outside.

Runa entered the habitat's airlock—the porch—hauling the supplies with her. The temperature plummeted twenty degrees. "Never gets easy," she murmured, sealing the door behind her, the porch pressurizing with a hiss. Head torch on, camera on, her mental check She held her breath and punched 'open.' Forty layers of frozen centigrade wrapped her like a jacket of ice. Every loose object was stolen by the hundred mile per hour wall of wind invading the porch. Head down, she attached her carabiner to the yellow lifeline and made for the dog yard, hauling the load. She stopped after twenty meters to yank the racing sled from its container and called his name.

Flint was a giant in size and reputation. He howled, his eyes burning with energy. "Go pick your team for the Outpost." She released the lead husky from his chain, allowing him to point with his muzzle at the fittest of them all.

Stooped against the storm, Runa tethered the team, one through seven, attaching them to the sled's bridle line. The remaining forty-three dogs were left howling in their rows of suspended kennels, their turn to stay home.

Last chance to check, she reminded herself. The huskies panted, pulling insanely against the sled, Runa's foot hard on the brake. No snow bridges. No short cuts. No cheating on turnaround time. Her mind processed the dangers, her body distracted by the storm. And in that second, it came to her. Flip from back-up to mains grid before I melt the generator. She scolded herself, dismounting to fix.

Runa hauled the snow anchors and lifted off the brake. "Harr mush!" She hollered, launching the team into the jaws of zone four.

12 Adventdalen

A strong wind at our back is best.
Bra vind i ryggen er best.
Norse Mythology

Runa did the math, yelling the facts to Flint. "Weather bomb's due in seven hours. Six to be safe. Turnaround time's half. So, if we're not at the Ark in three hours, we return to base. No matter what, where, or why, right Flint?"

Flint howled at the sound of his name, hauling the pack as if their lives depended on it, which they did.

Hounds and handler descended, paying homage to the mountain, edging along its switchback trail where the cliff face ended and the precipice began. Flint leaned hard to the side where darkness met whiteout, his fur brushing the ice wall.

"Wowa wowa, easy easy!" Runa hollered, stomping on the brake as the racing sled's momentum threatened to catch the team. I should have taken the slower cargo sled, she fretted, spying the Bolterdalen plateau ahead with relief.

"Gee!" Runa commanded. The team bore right, skirting the ghost towns and the long-deserted whaling stations, dwarfed by a backdrop of frozen fjords sparkling in the moonlight. As the storm regrouped, the sled's high-powered LEDs led the way, bathing the huskies in an eerie glow. The pack steamed and snarled, chasing Flint as he set the pace.

The wind rocketed them from behind. "Outpost, in thirty minutes—scratch twenty. *Bra vind i ryggen er best!* A strong wind at our back is best," Runa yelled defiantly at the storm, quoting from the playbook. In life, as in gaming, they had turned to the Viking Code enshrined in the book they swore to uphold. Its wisdom was timeless, its source a mystery to all but Runa.

The steel runners protested, surrendering to a glide as the team outran their lights crossing the notorious Adventdalen. Lulled by the hypnotic song of its razor sharp flats, she thought about the huskies and their bond, forged on the battlefields of ice and snow, each soul relying on the next for survival, moving as one, sensing danger as a pack.

"Big storm coming!" She hailed the team, broadening her stance on the rails. Tone, praise, and reward, secured their respect; talking to them was the secret. More than just huskies, they were her family—dependable, fiercely loyal. Runa smiled under her balaclava. You prefer their company to kids your age, Saskia's playful words echoed in her mind. For a moment, she thought about the mainland and her mood darkened. She punched the sled's bowrail as the guilt swept through her. "That was on me!" She yelled into the storm, startling the pack. If she'd handled the bullying differently, maybe it would have stopped. Perhaps they could have stayed. "Sucks being me. Harr mush!" She screamed at the memory, pushing the team harder still. Unlike kids, dogs were never cruel.

The double-headed axe of the North Pole. Its blades were as sharp as Viking steel. One threatening the mainland to leave her alone, the other smashing all hopes of traditional friendship. But even Spitzbergen's remoteness couldn't protect Runa from the rumors of her ancestry, following her like a dark cloud on the internet. At her worst, she'd felt lost, unable to think of the future, until the very thing that wounded her provided the solution—the ether. The exchange in the chatroom still fresh in her memory, she recounted how Groundswell had met, and the origin of their catchphrase.

"Gaming is Good!" Chase's anthem.

"In Moderation!" Hailed Scott, his adversary.

Chase Hudson versus Scott McMurdo in the PowerPlayers virtual forum. "Down with the imperial GameMaster!" yelled the duo, sinking the gaming conference, forcing the moderator to kill the debate.

Runa had liked, posted, and planted the seed of empathy with her new friends. The three eco-warriors converged, venting their frustrations in the dark corners of the internet. Kindred spirits were formed and Groundswell emerged like a phoenix from the ashes of their confidence.

13 Outpost

"Easy easy," Runa slowed the team as they exited zone four, frowning at the bullet holes in the warning sign. A bear in a red triangle: Keep Out/Danger of death. Written in three languages.

The howl of the wind competed with the husky's excited barking as they arrived on the Jannson Haugen Plateau.

"There!" Runa hollered to Flint, scanning the horizon, spying the zone three reflective marker. Same beast with an amber triangle and Russian wording: *Ne Puskat!* Out!

The explosion of halogen hit them first, blending white air and iced land into a single frigid haze. Brutal, dazzling spotlights tracked the incoming party from a thousand yards out.

"Easy easy whoa," Runa dabbed the brake, bringing her team to a controlled stop. She checked the time on her radio. Quick in and out, she promised herself, tossing the sled's anchors upwind. "Hide!" she commanded, and the huskies scratched shallow holes, forming fur circles, muzzles under tails, leaving only their eyes blinking in the snow.

Runa threw on her crampons and leaped off the sled, its frame shielding her actions as she grabbed *Chirp* with mitted hands. The dogs eyed their master kneeling next to the sign, pawing at the frigid ground like one of them as she placed the device at its base.

And now for the drop, she checked off in her mind. She reached for the mail package with numb hands and leaned into the blizzard, trudging the ten long meters to the outpost. She shielded her eyes against the paranoid searchlights, grumbling with every step as the lights hampered her night vision.

These guys have annoyed someone big time to get stationed out here, Runa reminded herself, wading toward the battered outer door. But like all Norwegians, she believed in people. And despite the secret she knew one of them kept, he deserved a second chance.

I should have worn snowshoes, she cursed, now up to her waist. The storm tore at the package as she paused to survey the old trappers' shack. Commandeered by the Barentsburg mining corporation for its perimeter security crew, it defined desolate.

Runa looked for signs of life as she dug for the handle, praying the bear-killer was asleep. When she found the entrance welded tight with ice, she prepared her shoulder and made to remove her rifle. *"Nei!"* She cursed, realizing it was back on the sled. She vented her anger with a shunt against the old oak panel, unsuccessfully. She stepped back, lunged, and kicked the door at the exact moment the searchlights died.

The driftwood porch was invaded by whirling snow, coating her prone figure as the outer door flapped viciously. She knelt and hit it again, silencing the storm, immediately regretting her recklessness as her head torch died, plunging the hall into darkness. Her senses heightened and her nose twitched at the smell of cordite, alcohol, and feet. Her eyes slowly adjusted, helped by a small candlelit porthole in the main cabin door.

Where's the package? she fretted, searching on her hands and knees between rows of fur boots, ropes, and rifle butts, locating it behind a pile of discarded glass bottles. The inner door sprang open with a crash. Runa scrambled to her feet as the silhouette of a giant holding a glowing metal bar blocked the entrance.

"Eto ya, eto ya! Sergei." It's me, it's me! Runa exclaimed, removing her snow plastered balaclava. "My Russian is not so good."

"You speak Russian better than useless Boris," Sergei said heartily, pointing at an equally large man snoring in an armchair. "All he's good for is drinking. Can't even stoke the fire."

He poked the coal, beckoning Runa into the warmth, wafting away the smoke. Orange flames cast eerie shadows over the mounted trophies of the trapper's trade and the bear killer sleeping in the seat.

"Get in before you freeze," he urged the embarrassed-looking girl before bombarding her with questions. "Have you brought it? You haven't lost Sergei's mama's most precious birthday cake? Why the sad face, Little Wolf? I get her to make it gluten-free—no wheat—*da*?"

"It's right here," Runa presented the flattened box from behind her back. "How could I forget your special day? Half a century old. The card's from me. I made it at school when they opened last week between storms."

"You are an angel, Runa. Too smart for school. You run country soon. But no stay, take slice with you. Big northerly is coming early. You must leave now for the Ark." The giant Cossack noticed she'd arrived unarmed. "Worries me to see you without rifle—no use leaving it on sled. Take mine, we have plenty. Saskia would skin me like a seal if anything happened. She reminds the world of this on the radio. I think she likes me."

Runa smiled, warming her hands in front of the fire, careful not to wake the bear killer. Sergei had a good heart. He was also the eyes and ears of the danger zones. If anything out of the ordinary happened out there, he would know about it, and so would she.

The room shook and flames flickered as a gust wafted soot down the chimney, filling the room with an icy chill. Sergei checked the sleeping man before speaking. "There is much new activity in zone four around the Svalrak launch site, a day's sail from here."

"I know where it is," she acknowledged, prodding the bear killer's foot.

"The American spacemen are drilling. Still searching in the wrong place." He chuckled.

Runa's expression didn't change. NASA had been launching sounding rockets up north in Svalrak since before she was born. Her mother worked for their launch partner, ESA, providing radar support when she wasn't studying space debris. NASA were the *good guys*. It was the others that concerned her.

The giant Cossack's expression changed. His voice sounded burdened. "You be careful, Little Wolf. We've had problems out here recently with the Russian mercenaries—pirates."

"Everyone makes mistakes, Sergei," Runa said defiantly.

"The life before. Da," he replied, his conscience reformed by his time in the Outpost.

Runa felt his pain, followed by a wave of guilt for mentioning his past on this of all days.

"Promise me you'll stop Boris shooting at the bears," Runa changed the subject, looking toward the sleeping guard sprawled in the seat. "Melting sea ice means they can't hunt the seals. They're forced to stray out of zone. Blame global warming, Sergei."

"His grudge runs deep. He was lucky to survive the attack. A survivor's never the same again. They fear their own shadow. It is why he drinks to forget. I will talk to him again."

Sergei's tone darkened, returning to the talk of mercenaries. "Armageddon," he used the sinister name the Russians gave the Ark, her destination. Its meaning: the place where the last battle on earth would be fought. He corrected himself quickly. "The Ark, it holds a prize more valuable than gold and diamonds. *Var forsiktig*, be careful Little Wolf. Go now, before the weather bomb hits."

Runa reflected on his warning before leaving the warmth of the room, refusing the rifle and stowing the cake. With the sound of him radioing the Ark from behind her, and the prospect of a fresh avalanche ahead, she gripped the outer door with both hands, waiting for Saskia's voice. The abrupt exchange ended with Sergei's apology for Saskia's verbal abuse. She does like him, Runa smiled, pulling down her balaclava.

"Out!" She hollered, approaching the sled. Flint's muzzle poked through the crust. His head followed, paws clawing, body shaking free from the snowhole. The pack copied. She hauled the anchors and released the foot brake. "Mush!" she commanded, sending the pack into a racing frenzy. "To the Ark, Flint."

14 Shrund

She who lives without discipline dies without honor.
Ho døyr utan ære som lever utan styring.

The huskies sensed it first, howling warnings amongst the pack. Flint picked up the pace without instruction. Runa felt for the rifle, making sure the gun slip was open. She shifted her weight to the left, forcing the racer to glide on a single rail, her right foot paddling against the rutted ice.

"It's early. Gee mush!" she yelled to Flint, turning the team to the right, willing them on. Her hands tightened on the sled bow as the threat surrounded them. The hairs on the back of her neck stood up as the barometric pressure bombed, popping her ears painfully. She felt for her talisman, searching her memory for a place to hide. Make for the Shrund, the head of the glacier, she thought Even the Vikings feared the place. A bottomless chasm, separating the ice plateau from the towering cliffs a thousand feet above; their overhang, Runa's savior. Too close would have them plunge into the icy abyss; too far and they'd fry in the lightning storm bursting above. *Fire or ice.* She remembered the warnings of the old Norse poems.

"Haw! We're taking a shortcut. Only a thousand yards more," she called, having flanked the massif for long enough. She veered off to the left, heading for the snow bridge and the protection of the overhang. But flouting polar rules came at a cost. *Ho døyr utan ære som lever utan styring.* She who lives without discipline dies without honor. The warning, from her deep conscience, forced a change of plan.

"Whoa!" Runa stomped on the foot brake and carved aggressively to a halt. She tossed the anchors and leaped over the front of the sled, sinking to her waist in deep snow, searching for the bridle line. She disappeared into the drift, digging for survival, finding, following, and freeing the line connecting the dogs to the sled. Her frozen fingers fumbled. The carabiner's clip refused her harness as the first strikes landed around them. She wrapped the wire around her waist and braced for the unthinkable, knowing the risks.

"Mush!" Runa shouted, cursing the sled's antenna and the risk it posed. A final look over her shoulder sealed it. But Flint didn'tmove, the lead pack dog defying the dangerous order. "Valhalla!" she roared, with Viking steel, desperate for distance from the lethal conductor. Flint took off, dragging the pack, launching Runa toward the Shrund.

Make a V! Stop the spin! she screamed to herself as the dogs hauled her headfirst towards oblivion. Her body cascaded through the snowdrifts, the line tightening around her waist, threatening to cut her in half as the team accelerated over the ice pack. Every rut, ramp, and ridge jarred her to the bone.

Runa twisted onto her back, and yelled, "Whoa whoa whoa!" Flint responded to the pain in her voice before the all-stop command, his full-tilt dive and roll forcing the team into a collision of huskies and harness.

Flint returned to his master's crumpled form, dragging the team with him. He snarled at the flashes of lightning, picking out the edge of the Shrund less than a sled's length away. The great husky sank his teeth into her jacket, hauled her body back from the rim, and probed it with his muzzle for signs of life. Runa stirred as the dog licked her face. Her eyes welded closed, she groaned, finding the bodycam wound tightly around her neck. She whispered to the huskies with her remaining strength, "Hide." But the dogs disobeyed the order for a second time, mustering around her, forming a protective scrum of loyal fur.

Ice lightning struck from all directions, illuminating the Shrund in the absolute darkness, bombarding the plateau with ear-splitting ferocity. The thunderclaps bounced the group like hailstones off a tin roof, as Mother Nature unleashed her anger upon them, launching, crashing, and smashing pure bolts of energy against the face of the Massif, demolishing its overhang. Rock and ice cascaded into the mouth of the Shrund, hurtling past the huddle into the abyss below. Its vacuum sucked them towards the edge. And then it hit. Every hair on every body stood vertically as a million volts of raw electricity impaled the ground, leaving the air crackling around them.

The smell of singed fur and husky breath was the second sensation Runa registered after the pain in her hand from clenching the talisman. Her eyes opened, spying the burning antenna. Dogs and human self-checked, rebooting. They stared at each other, the dogs panting. Runa shivered. Too close, she scolded herself, reaching for Flint.

She watched the lightning storm thrash its way out over the glacier as if chased by the devil himself. The stench of burnt plastic followed her as she trudged back to the sled despite the tearing wind. Discovering her jacket was the source, she rolled in the snow next to the charred remains. The aerial had taken a direct hit.

Runa replayed the checklist in reverse as she circled the sled wreckage, touching the blackened rifle, lights, GPS, and radio, all fried. It makes us deaf, blind, and defenseless, she thought. But at least we have cake, she smiled at the dogs, kneeling to offer them each a crushed morsel.

She reached for the bridle carabiner and looked at the wreckage. One of the sled's runners had survived. "Hallelujah, we're back in business, Flint! In this state, if we keep the lights of Longyearbyen on our right, we'll be at the Ark in sixty minutes."

The huskies pawed the ice restlessly at the sound of their home from home, eager as Runa to flee the unforgiving place. The team launched the moment her hands gripped the remains of the bowrail, dragging the mangled sled and making for zone two.

The crystal blue light of the Ark's entrance called to them, the wedge-shaped structure jutting out of the mountain like the tip of a concrete iceberg, its mass descending deep into the black rock where vaults hid its precious secret from the white world outside.

The security cameras twitched as she punched the intercom on the fortified gate. According to its clock, she was five minutes past her turnaround time. The Russian of Saskia Galin billowed through the speaker, forcing her to take a step back. *"Gde vy byli?"* Where have you been, little one?

"I can explain." Runa's voice was hoarse, barely audible.

Saskia's voice was a mixture of concern and relief. "I tried you twice on the UHF, but nothing."

"It took longer than expected to cross the Spitz glacier—the Shrund," Runa replied.

Her mentor's silence confirmed it would not be the end of the conversation.

"Please open the storm doors?"

Saskia lit up the checkpoint, startled by what she'd heard, dismayed by what she saw. "Oh, Mother Mary, I'm gonna kill Sergei!"

15 Armageddon

Let none put faith in the first sown field.
Lit ikkje på åker som er tidleg sådd.

The global seed vault. Crowned 'the Ark' by its Norwegian creators, codenamed 'Armageddon' by the soldiers of fortune; it was designed to deflect a nuclear blast, its defenses silencing the storm with ease.

The steel doors were ratcheted into the rock walls behind them by groaning pistons and whining hydraulics, the process completed with a pressure-sealing boom echoing down the tunnel, announcing their arrival. Panting huskies broke the silence—steaming and tails wagging, they vied for attention, finding their place as Flint howled order, his efforts interrupted by the smiling hologram. "Outer doors closed. Pressure equalized. Please proceed to the decontamination hall," invited the synthesized female voice.

Runa released the team from the wreckage of the sled, holding them as one by the bridle and staring down the ice-clad tunnel, thinking the unthinkable. If her hunch that NASA was behind The Game was correct, the space agency could be used to Groundswell's advantage. There was no way the good guys would allow Russian pirates to steal the Ark. But with no hard evidence of either, she was on her own.

The Ark's shaft resembled a Viking scepter, gradually descending twelve hundred feet, spearing the heart of the mountain with three dagger-like vaults. Each cave was fortified by a second blast door, each defending a priceless copy of the Global Seed Bank.

The hatch to the habitat swung open, snapping Runa out of her trance. Saskia, eyes wide, arms open, contradicted the hologram. "Dogs first. Explanation second!"

Runa relived her misadventure as she fed the huskies, omitting only her mission to conceal *Chirp* in zone three. The violence at the Shrund eclipsed Sergei's warning of Armageddon in the mind of her mentor. The radio squawked from the comms room.

"That will be Fraya. I'll talk to her first," Saskia said, throwing the remains of Runa's exposure suit in the trash. "Clean up. Meet me in the Oasis in thirty minutes. And if you think you're getting off your lessons—"

Runa scooted to the habitat, skipped the shower, and returned to the dog pen, relieved to find seven slumbering hounds fed, watered, and fidgeting, oblivious to the smell of their singed fur. Her heart quickened as she approached the hydroponics lab, nicknamed the Oasis, her hand hovering over the entry panel.

Whatever happens in the outside world, inside here I'm in control, Runa reminded herself, entering her favorite place on Earth. Greeted by the familiar cloak of humidity, she savored the release of tension as the jungle canopy revealed itself—tropical plants, flowing vines, flowers exploding color in every direction.

She absorbed her creation and sighed as if the world were weeping. Every living thing in the room had been rejected as imperfect by the Ark's crazy rules. She stacked the empty yellow incinerator crates, inhaled the aroma of a forest after rainfall, and caressed the exotic botanical plants.

"*Lit ikkje på åker som er tidleg sådd.*" Let none put faith in the first sown field, Runa whispered the Viking proverb. It had been the first entry in Groundswell's playbook, and the reason she vowed to protect the seeds— all of them.

The Ark's Norwegian creators had engineered redundancy. Three vaults. Three copies. Three chances to protect the world's crop seeds. But they were wrong. The botanical seeds were as important and it wasn't right that they were separated from the crop seeds and destroyed, she reminded herself for the hundredth time, looking around the Oasis. With the help of Groundswell, she would change things. But the Ark's rules were as clear as its space was limited: non-crops were out. No exceptions.

Runa stared at the source of the running water, the sound soothing her pain as it filled the hydroponics tank. She dipped her hands in the pond, leaning to care for the roots of the illegal plants, picturing her worries from the mainland drifting away on the current. This was her retreat, her domain, her calling. Of that, she was sure.

Her fantasy was interrupted by the talisman around her neck, drawing her attention with its habit of floating mysteriously like a dragonfly skimming the water's surface. She stared at its simple runic inscription, 'R,' meaning Journey. The Nordic birthstone had been in her family for generations. Every Norwegian kid had one, and most could recite the legend of its origin: *Fashioned from the stone that fell from the heavens, gathered in the thaw by the hand of the Viking. The runes etched by the steel of Eric the Red himself on the ice fields of Berget.*

Runa reflected on Sergei's warning. Her talisman was priceless only to her, but his talk of treasure, Armageddon, and pirates, lingered. And he would know, as he used to be one.

Runa's mood darkened, her inner voice warning of the invisible enemy. *Krigarar syner ikkje kva dei har på hjarte før øksa blottar det.* Warriors don't show their heart, until the axe reveals it. Her last entry in the playbook. This was a time for secrets. And Groundswell.

16 Oval Ultimatum

The President of the United States of America paced around the Oval Office. The most powerful man on the planet glared at the line of military dress uniforms, obscuring the row of technical experts awaiting sacrifice. His stare rested on the only civilian, as the tirade began. "Gentlemen, it sucks and it's Sunday. Deal with it! You know why you're here. What you don't know is how pissed I am with all of you. America's finest—Air Force Space Command. Navy Space and Naval Warfare Command. Army First Space Brigade—" he stepped closer to the only civilian, their noses almost touching, the President's spit landing on Director One's chin "—and NASA. Twenty billion dollars to you alone and I have to find out via social media that humans aren't biologically fit to fly."

"Astounding considering you run the country using the same media," murmured the professor from behind Chambers, the Director's sacrifice. Huck shook his head ever so slightly.

"Read my lips, people. I am one pissed president. I'm very, very angry! Fake news this is not, according to Dr Doom in WHO, a global genius agency based somewhere in Europe. Write this down people: the world health authority."

"Dr Woe, PhD, of the world health *organization*, Zurich, Switzerland," the professor said under his breath, agitated. "How did this guy become president?"

Huck shook his fist vigorously behind his back, imploring him to stop.

The President's rant continued. "You've thrown the keys for Mars to the Chinese and Russians! Nations that consider astronauts collateral damage in the conquest of space. Do you think they'll take their foot off the gas? Flags on Mars people, two years from now, and they won't be ours. I'm intelligent. Some would say I'm very, very, very smart. Yet it's me telling the rocket scientist: you should have seen this coming."

Allbright replaced the coffee lid noisily. The slurp of his super hot Lava latte the only sound in the room.

The President looked over his shoulder at his awestruck chief of staff, the fifth in as many months. The man nodded, scribbling, eyes widening as if his job depended on it, which it did.

"Double down, people! I promised my voters walls in Mexico and men on Mars. Listen very carefully. The elections are in twelve months, and I will not be a casualty! My voters will expect corrective action. Big action."

He turned abruptly, pointing with both hands, jabbing at the military ranks. "Special forces? We've just been ambushed. Caught sleeping on the job. And this just in. On my watch. As commander-in-chief, this makes me look weak, vulnerable. Unacceptable, people."

The generals looked as if they were about to confer.

"You three! Soldier, Sailor, Flyboy. As for your space commands, three will become one, and within twelve months. We're gonna make a single US Space Force. Consider yourselves singlified. Write that down."

The professor leaned forward and poked Chambers. "New word for you," he said, rolling his eyes.

The military brass swayed on the spot as if buffeted by a blast, looking at one another helplessly. Air Force Space Command was the first to protest, uttering only, "Mr President—" before being waved down by his commander-in-chief as he flapped his arms like a grotesque bird attempting flight, landing awkwardly in front of Director One.

"Listen up, NASA. There is zero, and I mean zero, political will to fund genetically flawed multi-billion dollar space programs. Crewed space flight is a thing of the past, canceled. Its budget will go to the newly combined US Space Force." The President stood, an insane grin transforming his face as he pressed his index finger and thumb together making the universal symbol for okay. "NASA, your monkeying around in space is over in twelve months. Gone. Yes, these two acts will appease the voters. Genius, pure genius."

Carrera's jaw opened, then slowly closed, leaving the only movement in the room his Adam's apple as he swallowed hard.

It was over, finished.

"Can't build your wall, but we can guarantee your re-election, Mr President." The words came from Huck Chambers, his small frame invisible behind Director One. His hand raised like a schoolboy.

The president stood with his arms folded, searching for the voice. "Speak using as few words as possible." Every eye behind the line of generals focused on Huck.

But it was the professor who uttered the words, in his trademark, authoritative tone. "Accelerated Evolution." He stood to his full height, his odd appearance the only introduction he needed.

"Where did this guy come from? Could only be NASA." The President pointed at the bearded man wearing the meatball hoodie. "Spare me the sci-fi babble. You have a ticket to ride for sixty seconds. Starting now!"

The professor leaned forward, speaking softly and deliberately. "Accelerated Evolution, Mr President, requires three ingredients: a child's body clock, physical preconditioning, and zero gravity. When combined, the results are magical. A scientific fusion of bone structure and immune system, creating the perfect body for deep space exploration."

The President looked unimpressed, pinching his chin as if in deep thought.

The professor simplified his pitch. "For the avoidance of doubt, sir, the future of NASA's human space flight program is about bodies and bones. And the solution lies within adolescents."

The shocked silence was amplified by the ticking of the Oval's clock. All eyes were on the president as if he were about to return a tennis serve. He unfolded his arms, clasped his tiny little hands, made a gun-like gesture with both index fingers pointing directly at the professor. "I get it, NASA-guy."

"At last," Allbright groaned a little too loudly.

"A kid's growth spurt in zero-G makes a super space traveler. I like it, like it a lot. This could seal my re-election, my second term. Hell, I could eclipse Kennedy by taking Mars. Can you prove this?" He demanded, pushing his way through the generals.

"Yes, Mr President. We have identified three suitable fourteen year old candidates. The proving ground is the international space station."

The president looked troubled for a second. "Dead kids don't get votes."

"Mr President, NASA's Mission-X program promotes survival."

"Guarantees!" The President demanded.

"Negative, sir. In the words of your predecessors, space travel is neither safe nor easy."

He paused to consider the professor's wisdom, Airforce Space Command seizing on the opportunity. "Mr President, we also have a team of adolescents. We have shadowed Mission-X, indeed supported it, our hand-picked superior air force candidates—"

His words were interrupted a second time by the man waving in a now-familiar way, looking delighted with himself. "What part of three-becomes-one do you people not get? Best of the best of the best? Gentlemen, smart voters will expect a combined military space team. Two tribes. One military, the other civilian. Genius, pure genius." He raised his hands, faced the dumbstruck audience triumphantly. "May the best tribe win! Mr ponytail," the President barked at the man from NASA who was deliberately ignoring him. "Hey, Dumbledore, how long do you need?"

"Twelve months," the professor replied.

"You got nine."

Turning to Director One. "Mission-X just became your top priority, got it?"

"Yes sir, Mr President, sir."

The president ambled towards the rear of the oval office, staring through the floor to ceiling windows, victorious. He pivoted on the spot and addressed the rabble. "Get to work! Everyone out. Especially you NASA bearded guy. Generals, Mr Civilian, don't move."

The room cleared quickly, as the rank and file attempted to make sense of the implications of what they'd just heard. The four men left standing stared at the President.

"For the avoidance of doubt, people," their commander-in-chief looked deadly serious. "In nine months, four jobs become one. Figure out who's in charge."

NASA's Director One inhaled sharply, his eyes widened, his career reborn.

17 Firing Room

Taking a new step is what people fear most.
Den største frykt ligg i det neste steg steg.

The two men waited in the empty foyer, shoulder to shoulder, watching the sunrise from Director One's layer. Space City's Building 1 was home to NASA's administration and the director of everything, its top floor the domain of Wade Carrera. Its frontage seamlessly constructed from glass, known as The Firing Room, it gave uninterrupted views of JSC's fourteen hundred acres, so he could see who left first.

Allbright was immune to the Director's power moves, and against Huck's advice, he'd disappeared after five minutes of waiting, torn between a Lava latte and a London fog tea. He Schwinn'd to Building 11, the source that fueled the most prestigious space agency on the planet, placed his order, and returned from NASA's canteen with nothing more than a reprimand for Friday's stampede.

"Come!" demanded the intercom. The professor led Huck, and the interns followed in a flying-V formation. The team found their direct route to Director One's glass desk blocked by a single uncomfortable-looking seat. The professor paused at the obstacle, shielding his eyes against the low sun, and surveyed the floor as if for traps. His team fixed on the bureaucrat as he fumbled inside a silver briefcase at his feet.

"Sit!" He ordered.

The professor motioned for Fox to oblige.

Wade Carrera spun around and waved a thick manila envelope. His eyes narrowed, irritated at the teenager sitting before him, his advantage lost. "These can't possibly be your team." He gestured towards the interns.

"Most astute of you," the Professor replied in his calm and measured tone. "The candidates, while identified, are neither aware of the responsibility awaiting them, nor acquainted with the sense of urgency."

Wade Carrera's palms squeaked against the glass as he leaned forward. Without fear of presidential repercussion, his thought train escaped. "The entire future of NASA's crewed space program. The president's political future. The lives of six kids. And you have promised our commander-in-chief the delivery of something not yet in your possession? Utter madness." The man's forehead inched toward the desk, his breath fogging his reflection in the glass.

The professor turned his back on the sunrise and the exasperated man. He spoke softly and sincerely, looking at each intern directly. *"Den største frykt ligg i det neste steg.* Taking a new step is what people fear most. A quote from the Groundswell playbook if I'm not mistaken. You, my friends, will secure our candidates and return with them in one week." Turning abruptly, he knocked on the glass desk, pointing at the envelope.

"You have until Friday to deliver your guinea pigs," Director One barked, pushing the bundle of paperwork towards the professor. "Three days will suffice. Failure to deliver defaults success to the military candidates. Sign here."

Cornelius Allbright dispatched the indemnity contract with a single stroke of his pen and left as powerfully as he'd entered.

"Go get your underdogs and be careful what you offer them," Director One said menacingly, hitting speed-dial.

"Air Force Space Command," replied the voice immediately.

"Get me the general," demanded Wade Carrera.

18 Viking

A bad rower blames the oar.
Han skuldar på åra som er ein dårleg roar.

The control room hummed its warning, surrounding Runa like a swarm of angry bees. Banks of computers drew power from reserves as the Ark prepared for a second meteorological hit. Her green and gold eyes studied the riot of red lights. The barometric pressure plummeted faster than a second counter—the classic trademark of a polar vortex.

Runa couldn't afford to get stranded in the Ark again—KHO's mountain top huskies needed feeding. Her mother knew it. Yet here she sat.

Runa relished the time with Saskia, but her mentor's tutoring was relentless, consuming every free minute. Her responsibility to feed the observatory hounds was the only guarantee she had to escape.

Where is she? Runa fretted, checking the station clock for the third time. She knew she had to leave immediately after Groundswell's videocall.

"I'm early," Saskia announced, relieving her protegee.

"Hi-bye." Runa acknowledged, racing to the radio room.

"Gaming is good!" They hailed in unison, after days of silence. The faces of Scott McMurdo and Chase Hudson flickered on the screen.

"Shouldn't you be at school?" Scott said, pointing at the rack of servers surrounding Runa.

"School's closed. It's fifty below outside. Have either of you heard anything at all?" she asked from deep within the mountain, willing there to be news about The Game.

"Well, that was an anti-climax," Chase said, answering her question with sarcasm. They could see him replace his feet on the desk, which was cluttered with gadgetry. Swallowing from a can of high energy soda, he belched, his eyes watering.

"Manners, Chase. Vikings present," Scott replied, half jesting.

"Nothing then," Runa sounded flat.

"Dude, at least you got comms back after four days of static. Must have been some electrical storm?" Chase asked.

"I've seen worse," she lied.

"I read it took out every transmitter in Spitzbergen?" Chase looked impressed.

"We all need to hang tight, as Mariner would say," Scott looked to Runa for a reaction, receiving none. "Groundswell's membership has trebled since we bombed out the finale. Let's agree on tactics and capitalize on having millions of new environmentalists. It's bound to help your plight, Runa, with the Russian mercenaries?"

"The Ark's running out of time. I can feel it. I just can't prove it," she sounded irratated.

"Well, whoever's behind The Game, we've got their attention now." Scott said.

Runa looked unconvinced, battling her lingering doubts. It had been months of hard work, simply to reject the prize money that their movement needed to promote Groundswell's cause and the Ark's jeopardy.

"Sounds like Scott's bought into your Russian conspiracy theory," Chase said, grinning and then changing the subject. "How's the new *Chirp* working out? Manage to plant it in zone three yet?"

Chirp had to be handled with care, having landed the trio in trouble with the authorities. The Navy proved dolphins could use their sonar to distinguish between anything underwater. NASA had pioneered the source code to mimic the smartest mammal on the planet. But it was Groundswell who'd adapted *Chirp*'s sound card to do radical stuff for the environment.

"I'll post the bodycam footage from the Outpost tonight." Her voice deadpan. Her bones still ached from the Shrund. "The first generation still works well. It's just the power source. Saskia says I need to keep a lower profile, especially with the tourist police. Too much sneaking around replacing batteries. No polar bear sightings in zone one or two this month. They're getting suspicious. It forces them to reduce the attack threat level, scale back their patrols, and take a hit on overtime. And then there's VisitSvalbard—the tourist board. No sightings means negative feedback and a drop in visitor numbers. Even Longyearbyen *lokastyre* complained about the lack of trade when I fetched KHO's supplies."

"*Chirp*'s just too cool," Chase couldn't hide his enthusiasm for the illegal tech.

"It's how we got hold of it in the first place that worries me," Runa said. "One of these days, it's going to bite us."

"You worry too much, boss. That one's on my dad. And his Seal team." Chase opened another can of soda. "Scott, how's *Chirp* working in Varrich Estate? Keeping the deer off the Mellness launch site?"

Scott frowned. "You had a nerve reprogramming *Chirp*'s transmitter to attract sheep instead of scaring deer. For twenty miles, every damn beast followed me like kids to an ice cream van, jamming the village center. We'll say nothing about your folly with *Chirp* and the Royal Norwegian Navy Chase!"

The two friends exchanged rude hand signs at the screens as Runa hurriedly packed for the trip to KHO.

"Hey Runa, nothing compares to your anti-whaling stunt," Chase shouted, ending the playful quarrel.

She immediately forgot the storm outside. "I blame your dodgy magnet, Chase," she countered. "I'd never have got caught if *Chirp* hadn't slid above the waterline."

"A bad rower blames the oar. Your wisdom in our playbook," Chase heckled.

"Han skuldar på åra som er ein dårleg roar." She repeated the phrase in Norwegian. He was right—he almost always was—despite using humor as his armor.

"What did the Norwegian whaling fleet brand you in the local press— Svalbardposten—Polar Nightmare?" Chase wiped his eyes. "*Chirp* emitting whale distress sounds ruined their catch for weeks."

"Months," she grumbled, staring into space. "That stunt gave me a free pass to the governor of Svalbard, Odin Berg. He said I had more lives than Lucky Leif Erikson hanging off that whaler in winter."

"Lucky who?" Chase asked.

"The son and sole survivor of Erik the Red's mythical *campaign of American conquest*," she eyed the clock again. "Odin Berg was torn between pinning a medal on me and repeating history. Though he warned if I pulled another stunt like that, I'd follow in the footsteps of my ancestors and find myself banished to Iceland. Sucks being different. I'm just saying, I'm on everyone's watch list."

Runa had referred to her ancestry, so the timing of Chase's news was perfect. His humor vanished. "About the thing. Your genetic link to the infamous Viking marauder, Erik the Red."

"Alleged link," she retaliated, lowering the checklist, wincing at her reflection in the polished steel door.

"The legend—you and he share the same exotic eyes. It's been the problem all along, right?" Chase's American confidence wavered as he skirted the edge of her woes. "The reason for the stuff on the mainland, the bullying. And the nightmare?"

"Always trying to help," Runa replied uneasily.

"I can make it go away," he announced triumphantly.

"You've got my full attention," Scott said sarcastically, as Runa turned her back on the camera.

"Not me. The captain of the Harrier." Chase grinned as he referred to the dive ship he called home. "Gotta love life on the high seas! In the spirit of exploration, Captain Voss takes on a not-for-profit job every year. This year he's followed his heart. Calls the operation *Red Legend*. He's convinced he'll prove his Viking ancestry, and in the process, Runa, disprove yours."

"You've lost me, Chase," Scott sounded confused, as Runa pretended to pack.

"He's hired a naval historian from Norway. The guy arrives in a few hours. Did you hear that, Runa?" Chase asked, looking puzzled, perhaps at why she wasn't sharing his enthusiasm. "According to Norse mythology, Erik the Red's fleet was lost in a storm returning to Norway, laden with evidence of North American colonization."

"I've heard the myth a hundred times," Runa said without looking up.

Chase raised his voice. "The Viking king of kings. The most fearsome marauder in history. Over a thousand years ago."

One friend was riveted while the other donned her jacket.

"Disprove this and the rest is nonsense. Right, team?" Chase's pitch was met with silence. "There's almost no sea ice this year in the Labrador straits due to global warming, so Captain Voss figures it's the perfect time to go ghost hunting."

"Cool," said Scott, his screen flickering.

Chase's drive to help Runa's life-long struggle to escape the stigma of her infamous ancestor was matched only by his desire to break out of his father's shadow. "I'm going to be the one who cracks the riddle of the Viking in our playbook," he insisted.

"The Viking code is nothing more than a code of ethics we play by," said Runa.

Chase's image flickered. "Yeah, but it's thousand year old gameplay. Viking wisdom forged in myth and legend, and you were raised on it. And you're hiding something in it, right? Let's see what we find off the Labrador coast. Hopefully, nothing." His chair skittered across Harrier's radio room as the ship steamed towards the dive site. His voice sounded burdened.

Runa stopped packing at the sound of silence and gave the screen her full attention. Chase stared at a tribute picture of his father, clearly unable to escape the man's reputation or expectations on the dive ship. "One day they'll see me," he murmured.

"I'm sure they will, Chase. We've all got history, and we all have to be careful," Runa said, feeling bad for ignoring her friend. He was only trying to help. She noticed Scott glance over his shoulder in Keeper's Cottage. "You too, Highlander."

Scott raised his hands at the camera. "And before anyone mentions my anti-plastic, crisp bag campaign—"

His plea was ignored by Chase as he lifted his head from the desk, his humor returning. "What? The mission that grounded the UK's Royal Mail. Yeah, better put that one behind you, dude."

"And where was my dad to help? On a bloody rig," Scott muttered.

Runa's attention shifted to the wall behind Scott. Its wood panelling was adorned with scenes of hunting, shooting, and fishing parties. Tweeds, rods, and the Keeper, his uncle Angus McMurdo. In every photo, he had his arm proudly around the lad. "Save that talk for another day?" Runa said, smiling limply.

"When you're ready, buddy." Chase offered Groundswell's three-fingered salute.

Runa zipped up her exposure suit. She faced the camera and slung the rifle over her shoulder. The Russian threat to the Ark was no conspiracy theory and she needed them to believe her. "Guys, listen up. Sergei in zone three sounded weird on Friday. Troubled."

"Who? The pirate?" Chase asked.

"That's behind him. Everyone deserves a second chance. He looks out for Saskia and me. He's a good man."

"Same can't be said about his buddy, Boris the bottle, the bear killer, right?" Chase shouted, waving his soda, froth foaming his keyboard, ending his call.

Runa turned to Scott. "With the increase of Russian and Chinese harbor traffic, and even NASA's activity at Svalrak, I've got this feeling. Can't shake it. Sergei was trying to tell me something."

It was Scott's turn for the connection to falter. "I'm losing you, Runa. News wires say the Chinese are making a play for Greenland's minerals, and the Russian Barentsburg mine has stepped up coal production. As for NASA, they're the good guys, right? Likely nothing in it."

"I hope you're right, Scott, because they're watching me. I'm convinced of it."

But the connection had already died, killed by Svalbard.

19 NASA One

NASA One made its approach to Svalbard, five hundred miles from the North Pole, fifty miles from Runa's location.

"Houston, this is NASA One. Landing conditions marginal. Forecast atrocious. Over."

"Copy that NASA One. Once on the ground, secure the plane, then hunker down for twenty-four hours. Over." The voice of Sky Symphony from Space City. "Intern One, do you copy back there?"

"Read you loud and clear, Houston."

Sky tasked the intern with her no-nonsense instructions. "Follow the brief. No shortcuts. Secure the friendly. Return home."

"Copy that Houston. Nice and easy. Evac for two, *maybe*," the intern replied sarcastically.

"Intern One, this time, it isn't a game. Houston over and out." She couldn't afford a repeat of the last rescue fiasco.

NASA One's chief pilot made the cabin announcement as he lowered his landing gear. "I'm gonna give you some advice. Do your gear-faffing, zips and all, before you exit. I've been here before in summer. When that gateway to hell opens, you're on your own, got it?"

The Lear jet's door struggled against the howling blizzard, fifty below and dropping. The intern attempted to exit, catching the full force of the storm. He clung to the handrails, sucker punched by the frigid air blast. Bent double, he descended in slow motion, one iced step at a time.

The co-pilot urged his only passenger to hurry, mouthing a four-letter word from the cockpit window as the cabin filled with snow.

The intern crouched on the bottom rung, like a diver finding his pool empty. The jet slid along the ice, rammed by the force of the wind, accelerating as he counted to three.

"Where's our guy?" The chief pilot asked.

"I shouted back. You heard me, sir."

"Nothing for it," the chief groaned, pumping the brakes, reaching for the throttle.

"Three, two, one—" yelled the intern, jumping the last inches onto the sheet ice.

"He's flat on his ass now," confirmed the co-pilot.

"Pray he stays down," urged the chief, throttling back, the scream of the engines matching the roar of the wind.

The intern slid under the wing. Like a hockey play on goal, the slapshot completed by the jet's engines, he was thrust like a puck without mercy, his body netted by the drift.

The intern looked for a point of reference through the darkness. Battered and bewildered he picked out the jet's dimly lit cockpit window, its fuselage already unrecognizable, painted with ice, its wheels anchored in the snowbank.

Fox Washington nursed his aching limbs, rolling over to investigate the orange flash closing on him through the blizzard. He stood with bowed legs, grasping his hood with one hand, the other outstretched as he skittered across the ice toward the source.

He raised his head at the *woosh* of the piston-activated door, sighing at the sound of a human voice.

"*Welkom*," the bus driver's gruff greeting. "You and your fancy red jacket better get in. Before Spitzbergen kills you."

20 Playbook

Runa raced to the Ark's reserve sled, grabbing only what she needed from the radio room, cursing as she spied the clock.

The call had taken too long and Chase was getting too close to the riddle of the Viking—the code contained in their playbook and the nightmare from where it came. It was threatening to unravel everything.

The same thing, every night: sleep, wake, scream. She wrote the wisdom from the nightmare in a dream diary, trying to make sense of it all. But letting the wisdom creep into their playbook had been a mistake. It helped their gameplay, but it didn't help her.

Fraya Erikson gave three chances. Runa was already at two. Her next misdemeanor would land her in the kommune boarding house at sea level, bunking with the miners' kids. If she missed her turnaround time or neglected the KHO huskies, she'd face the consequences.

"Minimum weight!" She yelled at the dogs, choosing *Chirp* and the bodycam over the rifle. She visualized the eye of the polar vortex arriving in two hours and fretted at her turnaround time. She computed the fastest route: across zone two, skirt Longyearbyen's outer limits, ascend the observatory's switchback trail from the north. Sixty minutes tops before I can feed the marooned huskies.

While the journey was routine, the margin for error was zero.

"Back!" Saskia Galin yelled up the arrivals tunnel, the echo emphasizing her urgency.

Runa was torn. Her hand hovered over the storm door emergency release—the wrath of Saskia versus the punishment of Fraya.

The huskies howled, writhing against the bridle as she jogged back to the habitat. If she got grounded, at least she'd still have the Oasis, she convinced herself, dreading the call to her mother at the radar station.

The pair exchanged glances as they listened to the situation developing over the HF radio. A conversation between Longyearbyen's only taxi driver and the tourist police. Half in Russian, the rest garbled Norwegian. All radio etiquette abandoned. The driver repeated his story at the demand of the disbelieving officer.

"The American was adamant, insane. Take me to the Ark, he demanded. Only two roads in this town, I told him. And this one just ran out. He said he'd walk the rest. Suicide, I told him, even in summer. American was wearing a red jacket, big NASA meatball on the back. He waived a GPS in my face, fancy-looking. Flashlight, but no rifle. He kept saying the future of space depended on him getting to the Ark. Watched him in my headlights disappear into the blizzard. Was sure he'd turn back. So, I waited. Was trying to raise you guys when old Thor crossed the road, all one thousand pounds of him."

"We'll take it from here, *da*," said the tourist police. Too casually for Runa's liking.

Runa grabbed her backpack. "Open the storm doors in sixty seconds. I'm going to save Thor."

"The hell you are!" Saskia reached for the radio. "That bear hasn't eaten in weeks. Do you forget you're fourteen? Leave him to the police."

"I was afraid you'd say that," Runa said, bolting the latch, jamming it with her carabiner, and hitting the storm door release.

"Harr mush!" Runa leaped onto the sled, dragging the anchors wildly, launching her team into zone two.

"Your rifle!" Saskia's anger was lost to the sound of the storm invading the tunnel.

21 The Pit

Fox Washington turned his back on the wind that was assaulting him, crouching to check his GPS, shaking the device awake. It looked like he was still on the transport road, invisible but for the snow pole tips flanking it. The distance to his destination was only one mile but a short cut was possible according to the display which was also warning low battery. The direct path, bearing ten degrees from his exact position, beckoned him—half the travel distance and straight to the Ark's control tower.

He gave the GPS a final shake and checked the route, the temperature icon now joining the power icon, flashing, beeping, and then dying. "Goddamn place!" NASA's intern yelled to no one, grabbing the old school compass tied around his neck. He dialed in the bearing, searching for a reference point through the white darkness.

Fox considered his second life-threatening decision in as many hours. Rely on his head torch and follow the snow poles, or take the short cut? His attention was caught by a glint of blue light. The second flash sealed it. The glint lured him onwards.

The snow softened the further he strayed from the transport road. The blizzard strengthened, obscuring all but the faint heartbeat of light as he felt his way through the darkness. Three steps forward, two back, head up to spot the flash, repeat. "Gimme a break!" he yelled at his own decision as much as the insane wind that hampered his progress.

The blue glow of the Ark's beacon teased, goading him to wade on. The destination in sight, his stride extended and he leaned into the storm, falling. His front foot pierced the crust, his back foot following. He snowballed down the incline, the ice chute ejecting him into The Pit.

The noise hit him first.

He searched for his flashlight, finding only the string to the compass, his eyes forced to adjust to the darkness.

Spitzbergen, a coaling station for over two hundred years, was littered with abandoned mines. The entrances were only visible during the summer melt, each marked by a single sign: a red triangle with a falling man screaming *FARE!* DANGER. The Pit was the most infamous of the mines.

Fox heard the gnashing of tooth against bone, the sound of frenzied feeding, amplified by the snow hollow.

He stared in horror at the blood-red polar bear, its jaws gnawing at a frozen limb swinging from a pole.

He was downwind of the predator, buying him vital seconds. His heart pounded over the storm, the beast so far oblivious to its next meal. Fumbling for the flares in his chest pockets, he fired two.

The explosions advertised his arrival, a haze of sparks and smoke surrounding his body. He was paralyzed, regretting a third decision that morning.

The blood-soaked bear recoiled, then rose to its full height of ten feet. The King of the Arctic surveyed his potential attacker and powered towards Fox on his hind legs, roaring his battle cry over the wind.

"Don't run out on me now!" he yelled at the flares. "Burn burn burn!" He backed away, gloves smoldering, the flares reduced to sparklers.

The beast landed on all fours, eyeing his warm meat, roaring louder than the storm, beginning his death charge.

Fox backtracked up the ice chute, holding nothing but a glowing baton in each hand. He faced his foe, pointing the dying embers, fixing to stab the predator's eye, mouth, tongue—anything—with his last ounce of strength.

The beast gained, its jaws widening,

Fox's nightmare worsened as a blizzard of wolves attacked from nowhere, tearing between him and the bear.

"Mush mush!" A girl's voice commanded, with the storm screaming behind her. One arm extended, she committed the wolves to the insane maneuver. The sled launched with impossible speed and angle, clearing the crater's edge. Its payload released mid-flight as the pack crunched chaotically against the ice of the transport road.

A diamond-white flash, followed by a sonic boom, forced Fox to duck and cover. Old Thor transformed into a thousand pounds of rolling rage and vanished into the darkness.

Fox lay deathly still, his eyes closed and his ears ringing. He was gasping and soaked in sweat, but alive.

"Mush!" The voice yelled again, and the girl looked over her shoulder at him, disappearing as suddenly as she'd arrived.

Two heavily armed tourist police veered off the transport road above, sirens wailing as their snowmobiles raced to the warning sign already stored in their GPS.

Fox dared to open his eyes. He lifted his head to stare at the blood trail next to his face just as his body was bathed in blue flashing lights and two other figures appeared.

"I have insurance," Fox yelled in gratitude over the storm.

"Where is *da* bear?" The first officer shouted impatiently in broken Russian. "Which direction?"

"You guys shot it, right? Saved my ass."

The second officer grabbed the intern's red jacket, pulling him close. "We not shoot *da* bear. *Dat's* not its blood."

Fox hurriedly self-checked, limb by limb.

The officer gestured to the snowmobile. "Get on, before you try dying out here again!"

His colleague disappeared into the mine, dragging the remains of the frozen deer the bear had been feasting on, hiding the evidence. He returned to recover the blood-soaked chain that swung from the warning sign and pointed at the tracks in the snow.

"Little Wolf!"

22 Melt Down

"For Odin sin kjærleik!" For the love of Odin, she cussed, unleashing her anger on the polar vortex breaking around them. She was more furious with herself than the foolhardy tourist in the red jacket or the police up to their usual tricks. Missing her turnaround time was inexcusable. "Wowa!" She commanded the team, stopping to inspect the damage from the rescue.

Runa pressed the talisman to her lips. She could see KHO's beacon, and felt the huskies' hunger, picturing the confrontation at either end.

The way she'd left the Ark would take some explaining, but it was KHO's marooned huskies that concerned her. With mother, it's three strikes and I'm out. Saskia, I can talk around. "Mush!" she hollered, choosing the plight of the dogs.

High on canine adrenaline, the hounds attacked the slope, fueled by the encounter with the King of the Arctic, a dog's worst enemy.

"Harr mush!" She yelled, venting her fury on the mountain, riding the sled on its one good ski. She replayed the incident, cussing the red jacket and nursing her team home.

Runa plotted. The vortex static would kill all comms—it always did. I need to diffuse the situation at the Ark en route, she thought. Others will be listening, especially mother. Make the call, her conscience demanded.

Her left leg trod the snow, paddling the buckled sled up the mountain, helping the dogs. Her right leg balanced on the good rail as the storm rocketed around the Breinosa Mountain, threatening to rip them off.

"Ark, this is KHO mobile, do you copy? Over." Runa shouted into her hood.

"State your position? Over." Saskia's response was immediate, curt. It had taken her ten seconds to kick the habitat's door free, but she'd been unwilling to risk closing the storm doors on her protégé.

"I'm thirty minutes out from KHO, please don't be mad at me Saskia. Thor survived, and so did the idiot Red Jacket. I left him at the Pit with *Chirp*."

"This isn't finished, Little Wolf. Report back upon arrival. Ark over and out."

Runa approached the summit. That's not right, she thought. KHO's brilliant white beacon pulsed dark orange. "*Nei!*" She yelled, punching the sled's bowrail and startling the dogs. I left the back-up generator on! She looked in the direction of the EISCAT radar station across the chasm, picturing her mother's fury, realizing her mistake a day late.

"We're in the vortex," she hailed Flint, as they limped the sled into the mountaintop dog yard, tossing the anchors to slow the team.

Fix the station power, feed the dogs, radio the Ark, in that order, she checked off. Runa apologized to the forty-three starving hounds.

She clipped onto the orange lifeline. This is going to hurt, she fretted, visualizing the generator shack, edging along the wire as the wind topped a hundred, it's chill sixty below.

Too quiet. Runa wiped her frozen goggles and released her grip at the end of the line, praying for ice on the roof.

Ingen ting. Nothing. She crouched, shielded her face, and cracked the door open an inch. There was no smoke, but the heat hit her like a wave. Dry fire, she cursed. The diesel generator's exhaust was glowing in the corner. I'll answer for that, Runa pictured the consequences, but her thoughts were interrupted by the agony of the generator as it caught, spluttered, and stalled. Its death throes plunged the observatory into incriminating darkness.

She jammed the door open to vent the fumes. After a count of three, she held her breath, raced to the breaker, and flicked it over with the back of her hand, switching the station power to mains.

"*Nei!*" she yelled as nothing happened, lunging for the door to gasp clean air. The grid must be down, she realized. It would be six hours before the generator wwould be cool enough to try again. She clipped herself back onto the lifeline and pictured her future in the bunkhouse at sea level, thinking what she would do if she ever saw the red jacket.

23 Red Jacket

Fox's story checked out, much to the amusement of the custody sergeant and the group of officers huddled around the radio in Longyearbyen's police station. A small private jet had landed. It fit the description. The plane was hauled to a hanger, the pilots refusing to disembark, although air traffic control was insistent. The afternoon's entertainment continued.

"High-profile attacks are bad for tourism," the police chief said, breaking up the party, concerned about his promotion prospects. "Go back to where you came from," was all he said to the boy in the cells, advice from the governor himself.

"As soon as it is safe to do so," echoed his men, laughing maliciously and relishing the overtime, ejecting Fox back into the storm. The intern scoured the whiteout for transport. Within a hundred frozen meters, he'd found it. A TL6 Svalbard all-terrain vehicle. All muscle with Russian insignia, the monster truck on power tracks was parked outside the harbor bar.

"You better be looking for a milkshake, sonny, as you ain't getting a drink in here," the barmaid said, serving her only customer, an enormous Russian sailor.

Fox waited for silence as the HF radio competed with the jukebox blasting heavy rock.

The sailor turned to stare at the intern, gesturing at the radio with his glass and pointing at the NASA meatball logo.

"This is the guy, no? Mr Red Jacket? The American." He laughed, spilling the remainder of his drink and demanding a refill from the tap.

Fox glanced at the clock above the bar. Like the Agency, he was running out of time and rapidly losing his sense of humor. "Two hundred dollars to take me to KHO in the vehicle outside. Now." He waited for a reaction as the man swallowed the liquid. Receiving none, he repeated his destination. "Kjell Henriksen Observatory."

"I know where it is, kid." The sailor looked unimpressed, slamming his glass on the bar. "Vortex already hit. Nobody going nowhere today."

"What's it gonna take, man? The future of NASA's human space program—"

The big Russian slammed his fist, cutting him short. "*Den*, it's worth a thousand Yankie dollars, no?"

"Goddamn pirate," Fox muttered under his breath, carelessly showing his emergency cash.

"Thousand each way. NASA got deep pockets, no."

"You take AMEX?" In the five seconds it took the intern to respond, the bar shook violently, firstly by the wind, then by the big Russian's fist.

"Cash up front, Mr Red Jacket. *Den*, we go."

24 Weird Science

"You sure this is it?" was the only thing Fox had to say during the fast and furious journey to the top of the Breinosa Mountain.

Fox neither warmed to the big Russian nor trusted him, as they approached the domed building that showed no signs of life.

"There's another two-fifty if you wait here," Fox shouted over the idling engine and the war of weather outside. "For thirty minutes, okay?"

"Five hundred for fifteen minutes. You pay now. We're here," the big Russian pointed to the windshield as the TL6 rocked from side to side.

"Your mother would be proud of you," Fox muttered, handing over the last of his cash. He crawled out the rear of the TL6 and jumped from the cab. The vortex retaliated. Enraged by KLO's thousand meter elevation, it sent Fox flying and he sank to his neck. His arms slashed with the flashlight and he swam for his life as the drift consumed him. The big Russian shifted into reverse.

"Sonofa—" Fox yelled, kicking and heaving, as the taillights warned of clanking tracks.

He hauled himself up and out of the path of the TL6, lunging at the yellow line to avoid its tracks. The big Russian touched his watch and held his hands high gesturing for the American to hurry.

Fox wrapped his arm around the lifesaving cable, shone the light, and snatched a glimpse of the observatory's dome. His field of vision was limited to a few feet either side of the line. He passed between the rows of strange stilted boxes, staring at his boots as he battled forward, kneeling midway to catch his breath. He peered into one of the weird science experiments and the beam of the flashlight shone through a square hole. Two large yellow reflectors narrowed, followed by the sound of an unraveling chain—a savage growling from the boxes spread like a ring of flaming petrol around him. Two eyes became a hundred. The first to attack was a giant. The grey beast howled wildly, rocketing towards the intruder baring its teeth. Forty-nine hounds followed their leader.

25 One to warn

Odd, thought Runa as she tapped the dog yard sensor. The alarm flashed silently in KHO's radio room as the station struggled on skeleton power.

Saskia's distorted voice was still scolding her over the warbling radio, although Runa could tell that the worst of her mentor's lecture had passed, unlike the storm. That just left her mother at the radar station, her binoculars undoubtedly trained on KHO as it languished in darkness.

Silencing the alarm, she counted in expectation. "Three, two, one."

"Over," Saskia said, finally allowing her to speak.

"Jeg forstar." I understand. "Love you—yard alarm. I must investigate. Out." Runa raced to the porch.

"Take a rifle," Saskia shouted, but the microphone was already swinging against the wall.

She loaded the Tika T3 Lite with the first of three 150-grain bear rounds and clipped onto the yellow line. She clicked the safety off and wound the sling around her arm for stability. She edged along the lifeline. Visibility was down to the length of the barrel, and she heard the commotion before she saw it.

Runa caught a glimpse of the carnage through the blizzard. The dogs jerked and writhed like spinning tops against their chains, howling and snarling, surrounding the predator. She raised her rifle. One to warn. The explosion grounded the dogs with deafening effectiveness. RShe chambered the next round and lowered the muzzle to cover the target laying low in the snow, aiming at the blood-red patch.

She knelt for the shot and moved her gloved finger over the trigger, her view hampered by the shards of ice peppering her face. One to wound.

At what point her mind properly identified the threat, she could not be sure. There was movement, a noise, a flash of light, unmistakably human.

"Sakte!" Slowly! She yelled, lowering the weapon, making it safe, watching the figure get to his knees, still gripping the cable. His jacket glowed in the flashlight taped to her barrel, sending the dogs back into a fierce frenzy.

"Hide!" She commanded, causing both the intruder and the dogs to slump to the ground.

"Not you, Red Jacket!" With the muzzle of her rifle, Runa beckoned for the figure to advance. "Second time I've saved your life today. *Forlate nå! Slik du kom!* Leave now the way you came!" She tossed a double red carabiner at his feet and tugged the red lifeline, pointing to the lights of the waiting TL6.

The storm stole his explanation. Her response was a second ear-splitting shot.

Fox dropped to his knees, demoralized. He grabbed the carabiner with hands of ice and clipped onto the line at the third attempt. He shielded his eyes against the high-powered spotlights as they arced over his head. The big Russian had abandoned him on the summit.

26 Tourist Trap

Merely book makes none wise.
Berre bok gjer ingen klok.

Runa watched her captive raise his arms slowly and make a choice between her or the vortex as the tail lights of his conspirator disappeared down the mountain. The intruder jabbed at the NASA logo on the back of his red jacket. She edged toward the airlock and decided his fate, slamming the door in his face.

"Gotta be kidding me." The last words she heard as he beat his fists against the closed steel.

The teenager retreated to the dimly lit radio room, clutching her rifle, watching the last volts of station power ebb away, thanks to Red Jacket outside. Had it not been for him, she could have arrived home sooner, and saved the generator.

KHO protocol for armed intruders was *run, hide, fight.* For all other scenarios, *secure, contain, alert.* "Berre bok gjer ingen klok." Merely book makes none wise. Runa tossed the station handbook at the HF radio that was crackling nothing but static. Her thoughts were interrupted by the banging on the porch.

The most northerly inhabited station on Earth was now in lockdown. Population: two. In ten minutes, it would be one if she didn't open the outer door.

It would be hours before she could call for help. She clasped her talisman, placing the stone against her lips, and wondered what she should do.

Something didn't stack up. To leave zone one required a weapon. That was the law. Red Jacket was defenseless in The Pit, and now again in KHO's dog yard. What was so important that this guy would risk his life? Twice.

What to do with him locked outside in -60C? The solution was staring her in the face. Inmarsat, the crisis satellite phone. It should work, assuming it powered up. Scooting around the control room, she shut down everything except the heating, emergency lights, and security sensors. She fired up the satellite communication system and placed her palms on it, willing the LED lights to glow.

"Ingen ting!" Nothing! She yelled at the dead panel. Plan B, she conceded.

Det er ingenting som kallast dårleg vêr, berre dårlege klær. There is no such thing as bad weather, only bad clothing. She squeezed into a second survival suit and hit the shutdown button, killing all station power.

The only light in the rapidly cooling room was a single LED, blinking pathetically, promising to search for a satellite. Runa held her breath. *"Raskere!"* Faster!

No connection, it flashed, unsympathetically.

The double suits would keep her alive but were uncomfortable and restricted her movement. She waddled back to the porch, leaving her frustrations cycling with the sat phone. Her eyes adjusted to the darkness as she searched the lockers for weapons, tools, anything dangerous, and tossed them into the habitat.

She left a medkit, exposure suit, and ration pack, before glancing back at the internal temperature. The mercury had plummeted both sides. She sealed the inner door, jamming it tight with a dog chain.

Runa entered the habitat to find the Inmarsat phone blinking green-orange, warning 'Poor Signal' and showing one out of four satellite bars. She knew the uplink wouldn't last long as she dialed her mother at the

EISCAT radar station. Three unsuccessful attempts later, she tried Saskia at the Ark. The line hinted at a dial tone, crackled, teased, then flatlined. Three more attempts and her luck had run out.

"*For Odin sin kjærleik!*" For the love of Odin, she yelled at the dormant radio. She had no contact with the outside world. The storm's electrical interference had won. She held the talisman and hit the outer door release. The hiss of the pressure line above her head confirmed it had opened. Her eyes darted to Inmarsat. Its signal strength jumped to four bars.

She hurriedly dialed Chase and Scott, praying the connection would hold. The digital silence magnified the agony of waiting. Her anguish broken by "Gaming is Good."

"Y'all having fun at the North Pole?" Chase asked enthusiastically. "Two calls in one day! Am I not the luckiest guy?"

Relieved to hear his sarcasm, Runa grabbed the receiver. "Chase, anything unusual happening your side?" But her transmission went unheard. Communication was inbound only.

He can't hear me, Runa fretted as she waited for Scott's line. "Don't hang—" She shouted at the panel.

Chase kept talking, all too familiar with unreliable comms. Desperate to chat with somebody his age, he filled the silence with ease. "Man, why Inmarsat? Hope you're not paying the bill! Got no internet? Geez, are KHO's systems on the blink again? Just the usual fiasco at sea here. We're steaming towards the Labrador straits for the big dive. Operation Red Legend, remember? But we're short of a couple of bow anchors so they're cutting and welding on the fly."

"Chase!" Runa tried and failed to interrupt.

"Gonna be interesting with the weather kicking off. The Norwegian VIP's due aboard any minute. Kinda bad timing if you ask me."

Runa's line finally flashed green. "Chase! I'm dealing with an emergency. Standby for sixty seconds," her admission interrupted by a rush of air through the pipes above her head, indicating the outer door was closing. She grabbed the rifle.

Runa returned to the porch, and with her back against the sealed door, she tapped the glass three times with the muzzle and then waited. She declared her position at the sound of movement and knelt to point the weapon at the porthole.

The red-hooded figure stared back at her, his breath fogging the glass, a glove pointed at his NASA insignia.

"Move, and I open the front hatch again," Runa warned, backing up the corridor, listening to the exchange behind her.

Chase's machine-gun laughter confirmed Scott had joined the call.

"How many keyboards have you foamed his week?" Scott said, teasing his friend's love of high energy soda and aversion to water.

"Dude, that's rich coming from a vegan living with a family of gamekeepers."

"Vegans have the lowest carbon footprint."

"Vegetables are overrated," Chase insisted.

"Keepers get a bad rap. They love the land. Where's our gluten-free leader?" Scott asked before his wingman could counter.

"Busy winding me up," he replied. "No doubt it's payback for the flash-bang *Chirp* I sent her. KHO sounds like it's falling apart. No internet, no power. Those planetary research scientists need to start upgrading."

"Guys," Runa interrupted. "I've bagged an intruder in the airlock." The line went silent. Two bars confirmed the comms link was still up.

"Come again?" Scott's voice echoed, his connection deteriorating.

"Say what?" Chase's line warbled. "Runa, whatever you do, don't let the guy in. Call for help."

"Red jacket," she responded. "Bright red jacket."

"I'll call Ark and EISCAT," Chase clipped his words, predicting the line would fail any moment.

"Saskia's a trooper. She'll fix this Russian-style," Scott interrupted. "I'll target UNIS. The university of Svalbard specializes in hostile environment rescue, right?"

"All stop," Runa urged, the Satcom icon dropped to one bar. Red Jacket's antics swirled in her head. "He's going nowhere. I'll uplink the footage and you can see what you make of it."

But something didn't make sense in any language.

Scott dropped off the call.

"I can't reach Ark or EISCAT, but I'll keep trying." Chase's statement was cut short by Harrier's fire alarm.

"The Game," she murmured, the thought revealing itself as Groundswell's crisis worsened. The Game and the intruder were linked. He'd tried, he'd failed, and twice he'd referenced NASA. The good guys?

"Stay on the line, Chase," Runa shouted to the dead satellite phone. She edged back down the corridor and faced the porch.

Despite the insane temperature, the captive had blocked the porthole with his notorious jacket, its NASA logo squashing a business card against the glass. *The future of crewed spaceflight depends on you,* was scrawled across it.

Runa returned to the command seat. Leaning the rifle against the wall, she stared at the racks of dead technology and listened to the polar vortex punish the observatory. Just as soon as the grid was up or the generator was cool enough, she'd make the calls. She pulled on her hood and closed her eyes for a second. Her body craved sleep and was shutting down. Her last conscious thought was her fear of the nightmare, as she slipped into darkness.

27 UNIS

News traveled fast in the polar region. Everyone was listening.

Red Jacket—the source of all emergencies since NASA One landed—had made the American agency top of the Arctic radio waves for all the wrong reasons.

Scott's first call to the UNIS rescue center was dismissed as a child's prank. His second triggered a chain reaction.

"No way a kid in Scotland could make this up." The operator's hand covered the receiver while he beckoned his superior and switched to speaker. Both gasped at the mention of the intruder's description, repeating the color of the fateful jacket.

"He has to hear this," the supervisor insisted, patching the call through to the governor.

Minutes later, the governor of Svalbard demanded answers from NASA One. Its pilots still refused to leave the cockpit; the airmen neither allowed Berg's men to board, nor were they willing to divulge the name of the Red Jacket, although they conceded they were a man down.

Six armed and humorless men formed the UNIS rescue party. Mobilized in three Hagglund all-terrain vehicles, they vanished into the storm. Odin Berg's orders: Arrest that man.

28 Purple Flare

Saskia paced around the Ark's control room, hurling insults at the vortex. It had stripped the Breinosa mountain of comms leaving both KHO and EISCAT blind and deaf. A prisoner to the storm, she was forced to listen to soundbites of the story of Red Jacket unfold over the local airwaves— until the international cold call penetrated the static. She answered the ARK's emergency line on its second ring.

The fourteen year old American was adamant, the child's story too impossible to be untrue. His friend, Runa Erikson, was in mortal danger.

Saskia kicked the trash can, scolded the messenger, killed Chase's call, and launched the purple flares.

29 EISCAT

Fraya Erikson cursed the EISCAT radar station's radio for the umpteenth time, shaking her fist at the *no signal* icon. Europe's most powerful listening device had been rendered useless by the polar vortex as it taunted the Breinosa mountain. Runa's mother was hostage to the storm, incapable of calling Saskia in the Ark below until she caught sight of the last purple flare.

Fraya broke all the rules, maneuvering the giant dish into the winds, its screaming hydraulics warning of the quake to come. The radar's apex pointed directly at the Ark and the whine of the energy built as she reversed its signal polarity. The boom of EISCAT's sonic blast forced the Ark's comms panel to register four out of four bars. Saskia saluted her best friend.

The two women acted with Norwegian determination and the cunning of a Cossack, speaking in riddles to evade the eavesdroppers. One phoned ESA, the other hailed the Outpost.

Fraya broke the glass with her elbow, activating the emergency hotline to ESA. The European Space Agency answered immediately, its operator holding the receiver at arm's length as the planetary scientist filed her charges. Why had ESA's launch partner, NASA, arrived unannounced during a polar storm, targeted the Ark, and then held her fourteen year old daughter hostage in the observatory?

Fraya's plan set in motion, she was transferred to the source of the international incident.

Building 1 confirmed their asset NASA One, was on exercise at the North Pole. Fraya was advised to hold while Building 9 was instructed to talk to EISCAT radar station and sort out their goddamn mess.

Huck Chambers offered no apology during the five minute conversation with Fraya Erikson. Runa's mother listened silently, her jaw open, as the space agency replayed her daughter's accolades.

'Remarkable Runa' and her two best friends had earned the right to try out for NASA's junior astronaut program. At that very moment, the Agency was securing the trio of candidates. If successful, they'd receive a full academic scholarship, a guaranteed career with NASA, and be home in time for Christmas.

In the absence of questions, Huck continued with his script.

If Runa interviewed, NASA's partners—the KHO observatory and EISCAT radar station—would benefit to the tune of an unlimited budget for additional cube satellite launches and a new plasma telescope to study the Aurora Borealis. NASA hoped to sway Fraya and Saskia by offering both scientists incentives.

Huck looked at his watch, then the calendar. He left no doubt as to NASA's intentions as he threw his ace on the table prematurely. The Ark would receive funding for the creation of a fourth cavern to contain every botanical seed on the planet, in addition to the current food crops, funded for a hundred years. The agency's jet was standing by and would depart immediately upon Runa Erikson's and Fox Washington's arrival. It was a national imperative that the US citizen—and NASA employee—not be detained by the local authorities. The interview was in twenty-four hours in Houston, Texas. The offer was for two tickets, valid for sixty minutes.

Fraya relayed the once-in-a-lifetime opportunity to Saskia in full, omitting only the offer of two tickets, as her work always came first. As she spoke, she stared outside at the lights ascending opposite sides of the Breinosa mountain.

30 Warning Word

Seek Something, Risk Everything.
Søk noko, risiker alt.

Runa stirred as fans whirred, computers re-booted, and screens flickered, white light engulfing her as the radio room burst into life. Her dream diary was in one hand and her talisman clenched in the other. She looked at her handwriting and groaned. *Søk noko, risiker alt.* Seek something, risk everything.

How long had she slept? She scrambled to switch on the HF radio, catching Saskia's tired voice in mid-sentence "—KHO this is Ark, do you read? UNIS rescue parties inbound. Polaris. Repeat, Polaris," she said, cryptic to all but Runa.

"I read you, Ark." Runa was instantly alert.

Saskia had used their safeword—Polaris—the warning of imminent danger.

"Er du nær ulvens øyrer så pass deg for tennene." Where wolves' ears are, wolves' teeth are near. Saskia quoted from Groundswell's playbook.

Runa switched to the porch camera in time to see the ice-clad figure approach. She reached for the rifle. "Copy that Ark. KHO out."

31 Abominable Snowman

There was only one way into KHO observatory and that was through the airlock.

Fox Washington had settled for being alive. As exhausted as his options, he'd crawled under the pile of exposure suits and fallen into a dreamless sleep until his cover was sucked out by the Vortex rushing in.

"I did what you asked!" He protested at the camera through the twister of debris, finding his only exit blocked by a stooping iced giant.

He jolted upright, shocked as much by the rush of frozen air as the ghostly vision. He scrambled backward as the abominable snowman beat its body free of ice. Fox lay staring at the figure that dwarfed even the big Russian. Pinching himself, he prayed he was still asleep.

The station power flickered to reveal the frozen hulk clench its white weapon and tower over the defenseless intern. The giant menaced the prone figure, breath streaming through the holes in its iced balaclava. "Anything happens to Little Wolf, I find you, feed your eyes to the ravens, heart to the bears, liver to the dogs. Understand, NASA?" Sergei the Cossack stepped over Fox with one stride and removed the red jacket from the porthole, flinging it at the intern. "Get dressed. We leave in five minutes. Be ready."

32 Gifts

Runa reached for her rifle and investigated the sound of tapping coming from the porch, removing the chain at the sight of Sergei's face.

"Call your mother," he said.

Runa listened calmly over the secure link as Fraya launched into a summary of the space agency's gifts. Runa feigned surprise at the reference to NASA and waited for the part where she got grounded. It never came. The NASA monologue was interrupted only once as Saskia joined the call, warning of western promises.

Runa was suspicious. "—a fourth cavern for every *botanical* seed on the planet?" She'd shared her dream with no other living soul. How did NASA know about her innermost secret?

She panicked, feeling for the answer, searching for the evidence beneath her layers of clothing, sighing as she touched the edge of her diary, the original playbook. But how could they have read it?

Søk noko, risiker alt. Seek something, risk everything. Her thoughts collided. She was torn but tempted. The wisdom of the nightmare goaded her. Their environmental movement's fuel was controversy, its currency was gaming, and its growth was viral. Groundswell's call to action existed for this very moment.

Sergei broke the silence. "Pack your bag, Little Wolf; you're leaving."

"I'll give it my best shot." Runa's lukewarm response met with surprise and disappointment.

"Adolescents," Saskia said over the ether.

Runa flashed back to Season 9 and the rooftop exchange; her axe and NASA's hellfire. "Let's hope it doesn't end the same way," she muttered under her breath as she shuffled back to her cabin, encouraging Sergei to talk to Saskia, which he did eagerly.

Passport in one hand, rifle in the other, she joined the giant Cossack by the porch's inner door.

"Won't be needing that," Sergei said, pointing at the rifle, gesturing toward his Hagglund all-terrain through the window. The giant pulled on his balaclava.

His voice was full of reverence, his gamble registering with Runa. "But we must hurry. UNIS and authorities will be here soon. They'll arrest the Red Jacket and prevent our departure, which will madden Saskia. Their new vehicles are twice as fast as my trusty Hagglund, but I took her up the direct route. I followed mine seven's conveyor. Risky, but we return the same way, *da*?

"What about the dogs?"

"I'll move them to the public pound later. Don't worry; they like me, especially the big beast. And Runa, lose one of the survival suits."

33 Hagglund

Own only what you can carry with you.
Eig ikkje meir enn du kan bære.

Fox made for the outer door the instant the giant opened the inner. Runa gave him a look as cold as the storm outside.

"Is that it?" Sergei commented, on the lack of her belongings.

"Eig ikkje meir enn du kan bære. Own only what you can carry with you," she replied, feeling for the talisman and quoting from the diary stowed in her pocket.

Fox heard the girl's voice clearly for the first time. Candidate Viking. Everything depended on her. NASA was convinced of that.

Fox braced himself. A whistle replaced the airlock's hiss as the vortex emptied the porch once more.

"Leave the flashlight," the giant Cossack ordered over the explosion of noise. He waded towards the Hagglund, stopping to indicate to NASA to ride in the rear stowage cab of the tank-like vehicle.

"We go now!" he shouted, hood to hood with Runa, pointing at the convoy of headlights climbing the mountain.

The Hagglund defied gravity as Sergei hugged the coal conveyor, the fugitives descending the face of Breinosa. The four-point harnesses suspended the driver and passenger above the boxy windshield as NASA hung in the cargo cab. Fox snatched at the dangling headset, protecting his ears against the screaming machine as it battled the impossible angle in its lowest gear. He swallowed as he listened to the driver's mutterings.

"The direct route is our only chance of Red Jacket evading capture."

The driver's words were little comfort to the intern as he gritted his teeth against the vibrating tracks, convinced he was skiing down a black run in a metal coffin. "We make for the airport via harbor. Avoid roadblocks. I need to show you something, Runa."

The Hagglund crept off the Breinosa mountain and stalked its way onto the exposed Adventdalen ice plateau. Sergei switched the transmission to a higher gear, praying the sizzling engine would cool, and checking the wing mirrors. "Here they come."

The authorities descended at speed. High-powered searchlights probed the storm, scanning for the fugitive.

Sergei's face fogged the glass despite his perfect night vision as the fleeing Hagglund tore across the hard-pack ice at a bone-shaking thirty-four miles an hour. The noise of the tracks drowned the engine, the vibration shaking Fox to his core.

"Can this day get any worse?" he unwittingly yelled to the driver, as their pursuers arrived on the plateau and the race into deepening darkness began.

"Da!" Yes! Sergei grunted, unable to switch off the intercom. He pointed at the Russian icebreaker in the harbor, now a blaze of activity. He lifted off the accelerator, punching the dashboard as the crane landed trailers on the dock. "Look, see her bowline; she's empty. Pirates. No-good Russian mercenaries."

The authorities split. Only one followed the fugitives' tracks, their destination so obvious; the others veered towards the airport.

Sergei shook his fist through the back windshield, annoyed at having to slow the vehicle for NASA to hear him over the din of the tracks. His voice was threatening. "I know you are listening, Red Jacket. Switch to channel nine. Call your fancy jet. Make sure your lazy pilots have de-iced. Tell them to prepare for emergency evacuation."

The population of Longyearbyen joined the fugitives listening to the radio chatter between air traffic control and the authorities. A thousand yards behind and closing on Runa, they demanded the tower shut the airport.

Sergei swerved towards the snowblower tracks and wedged the vehicle into the dead-end route skirting the runway's perimeter fence. The snowdrift was level with the Hagglund's roof, leaving only the fence's razor wire exposed. "Jump and roll, Little Wolf!"

Runa climbed through the emergency hatch and Fox followed, gripping the roof rails as the wind pummeled them.

Lights raked the Hagglund and loudspeakers barked unintelligible orders in angry English.

Sergei squeezed his shoulders through the gap. "Red Jacket, remember what I told you. Eyes, heart, lungs!"

34 Exodus

"Negative, NASA One. Repeat, you are not clear for take-off. Return to the hanger immediately. Over," the air traffic controller demanded.

NASA One ignored the order, taxied illegally to the end of the runway and stood facing three enemies, mission failure being the worst of them. The jet was empty of passengers. Its fuselage shook and its engines screamed as the chief pilot battled thrust against brakes, preparing for a slingshot departure. The cabin was filling with snow through the door left open for the fugitives. The jet's steps protested. Acting like a sail, they gybed the nose of the plane downwind, two minutes before their forbidden departure slot.

The authorities reached the far end of the runway, fanning out like linebackers before the charge.

"Houston, this is NASA One inbound. We have a problem. Over." The pilots shielded their eyes against the wall of light charging towards them.

"Fix it!" Sky Symphony ordered from Houston.

"Go, go, go!" Fox yelled, scrambling inside the jet and grabbing the co-pilot's shoulder, Runa behind him.

"Man, you're cutting it fine! Buckle up!" the airman yelled, retracting the steps. The door closed with an icy crunch, smothering the noise of the carnage outside, the cabin filling with a new roar.

NASA's chief pilot traded safety over speed, releasing the brakes. His engines were already at half throttle.

"They ain't moving," the co-pilot observed, staring through the cockpit window.

"Neither are we." The chief pilot throttled back fully, committing to the two hundred mile an hour game of chicken.

"They still ain't moving."

"Goddamn Vikings!" The pilot yelled, dousing the jet's lights.

"Abort! Abort!" yelled the authorities over the radio, the recklessly committed jet now invisible. The tracked vehicles veered left and right, disappearing into the deep perimeter snow.

The Lear climbed at an insane angle, ripping a hole in the storm and banking hard to the south.

"NASA One, this is Houston. Confirm status. Over." Sky Symphony demanded.

"Houston, situation green. Achieved cruising altitude. Evac for one. Mission accomplished. Over."

The chief pilot switched to the intercom and addressed his passengers with an American drawl. "Intern one. Outstanding job, buddy. I didn't think you had it in you!"

Candidate Viking retreated into her jacket hood, its fur line hiding the suspicion on her face. She relived Season 9's rescue and issued her threat to the boy in the red jacket. "The future of crewed spaceflight depends on *you*. That's what you wrote. If my team—and I mean all of them—isn't waiting for me on the tarmac when I land, the deal's off."

35 Mariner

Chase Hudson slumped in the corner of the dive ship's radio room like a boxer flattened first round in the ring. Learning of Runa's jeopardy, the boy had done what any fourteen year old would—he'd phoned for help. Saskia had listened, blamed, and then flattened him in the few seconds the link was up. Her accusation of Groundswell's folly in the events at the North Pole left him in no doubt; she was both furious and capable of rescuing her protégée and his best friend. But her tone far from convinced him that Runa wasn't in mortal danger. Plagued by static, the call ended prematurely.

Chase was part of a nomadic community that looked after its own. Living amongst treasure hunters, he was a graduate of the school of loyalty, trust, and teamwork by the age of fourteen—cornerstones of survival in the deep sea diving industry. His work ethic and limitless curiosity were matched only by his burning desire to break free from his father's swashbuckling reputation.

Chase considered every challenge a riddle to be solved. He was always the first to volunteer and the last to quit, paying the price by snatching meals and sleeping randomly. He was a child immersed in an adult world, which explained his devotion to an online peer group and reliance on internet gaming.

He exhaled slowly, unable to reach Scott McMurdo to discuss the call. He puffed on his inhaler, instantly easing the stress of his breathing. His eyes darted between the radio and the figure turning sideways through the doorway.

Chase vacated the *Turtle Beach* gaming chair for the jolliest man afloat. "Nice threads, man." He complimented Hershey on his Season 9 3XL coveralls as he headed for the console.

Not once during the meteoric rise of Groundswell and its success within Season 9 did Hershey suspect that his young friend was one of the ringleaders. And why would he? Chase had sworn himself to secrecy under the Viking Code.

Hershey was far more than just the ship's radio operator and most fanatical gamer. He held a PhD in nanoelectronics from MIT. "Gaming is good," he announced, using Groundswell's catchphrase, making their heartfelt three-finger salute.

"In moderation, dude." Chase nodded towards the squawk box. "Gonna get that?"

"Hey Mariner, you touch anything when I was out?" Hershey used the boy's nickname; everyone on the boat had one and nobody got to choose it.

Anyone entering the radio operator's domain received the same question. A failure to answer honestly frequently resulted in acoustic injury, as the man was obsessed with sonic experiments.

"Dude, you need to cut back."

"Trying, man." Hershey gorged on a family-sized bag of *Doritos.*

Chase patted the pile of gaming magazines. "You know what I mean. Gaming's like ivy. It can smother you."

Chase played Season 9 for a reason—Groundswell. Hershey played because he was addicted. Everyone knew it, except for the wayward genius himself, and Chase was convinced he could help.

Hershey ignored the chopper pilot hailing Harrier. He reached for the mic, turned up the music, and tapped the clock, offering his friend some advice. "Mariner, don't blow your big day by forgetting to feed the divers decompressing in the bin." *The bin* was crew-speak for the dive chamber, the home of submariners. And there was none hungrier than dive superintendent Fingers Hudson, lead diver and Chase's father. The decorated military man's appetite for adventure and reputation eclipsed the ship and all who lived on it.

"Tell saturation control I'll be down with their chow in ten," Chase said with excitement, as he planned the fastest route from the galley to dive chamber one.

"Tell 'em yourself," Hershey replied, pointing at the flashing comms panel and the team keeping the divers alive. "Better make that five."

"Copy that," Chase confirmed, leaving Hershey to field the incoming call.

36 Milkround

"Harrier salvage vessel, this is Milkround Chopper One. Do you copy? Over." The radio barked.

"Milkround, we read you loud and clear," replied Hershey. "Man, we weren't expecting you until midnight. Over."

"You had us worried for a moment, Harrier," replied the voice of the seen-it-all, done-it-all pilot. "Son, we have VIPs onboard. Deep pockets. Paid for the whole drop, so we're high-tailing directly to y'all. Over."

"A-okay with us, Milkround," Hershey replied, air guitaring, mouth full. "As long as you have our spare parts and the deck boss's *Cinnabons*, you'll be welcomed. Over."

"Expected time of arrival, sixty minutes with the current wind speed. And we'll need to refuel. Over."

"Standby, Milkround." Hershey peered out the forward-facing window, distracted by the sound of ripping metal.

At three hundred and fifty feet long and forty thousand tons, Harrier was a formidable ship in any weather conditions and was making light of the Eastern Seaboard's swell. It was the commotion around the helicopter landing pad that concerned Hershey. The deck that perched above the ship's bow bristled with scaffolding and swarmed with brightly clad metal workers, their tools spitting flames high into the half-light of dusk.

"Copy that, Milkround. I suggest you reduce your speed by fifty percent. We're doing a little housekeeping. Over." Hershey stopped strumming and peered at the screen. "It's here," he murmured trancelike into the mic.

The all new Season 10 had arrived, announced the ticker-tape news flash. Season 9, the world's most addictive online game, had been offline since the hack a week ago, sabotaged by the environmentalists Groundswell. Hershey's gaze never left the screen as he counted the download percentage.

"Harrier. Our ETA ninety minutes."

Hershey kissed the screen and questioned the pilot. "Say what Milkround?"

"Expected time of arrival, nine-zero minutes. Confirm, ninety minutes Harrier. On fumes. Don't forget. Over."

With the chopper three hours early, deck repairs running three hours late, and Hershey's first battle scheduled in sixty minutes, it was going to be tight.

37 Licorice Water

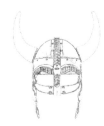

"You're late, Chase. What kept ya?" complained Coolio, the second most important person on the ship. The Italian Michelin chef from New York carried his title of 'camp boss' with pride. His food was as legendary as his wit, not to mention his linguistic ability. The only complaint in his galley was his temper when crossed.

"What national emergency is it this time?" Coolio sang the words as he prepared the evening meal. "Get this feast to the bin *pronto*. Steak Provence *ici*. Service *Vamoose*. And Mariner, blow the food down carefully, else you'll freeze it in the airlock. Avoid an earful from you-know-who, *capiche*?"

"*Capiche*." Chase balanced his payload as he descended the three decks to saturation control, arriving in the belly of the ship panting and blaming his inhaler.

The dive chamber. A pair of cylinders resembling two Airstream motorhomes bridged by a narrow tunnel. It was affectionately known as 'the bin' and was home to a dozen demanding divers for a month at a time.

No place of privacy, the dive chamber currently housed Fingers, Ace, and Blades—the last team and the most experienced. With each person's life in the hands of the others, the risks to the team were not unlike those of a lunar landing: one soul orbited—the bellman, while the other two landed—spacewalking divers willing to explore the seabed in the spirit of adventure.

Lead diver Fingers, Ace his bellman, and Blades his third in command had spent two weeks at one hundred and eighty feet and were nearing the end of a forty-hour decompression cycle called the *Big Blow Down*. They were demob happy and celebrating the homebound process.

Chase decanted the meals into aluminum containers before placing them inside the transfer airlock and blowing them down by equalizing the pressure. He announced its arrival in the customary way hollering. "Chow down!"

Two divers rushed to the portholes, squashing their faces against the glass, mouthing obscenities, as a third bared his ass.

"Saturation divers," Chase rolled his eyes, ignoring the childish behavior. "What kinda role models are you?"

Fingers grabbed the intercom, breaking into a painful chorus of *Leaving on a jet plane,* backed by his buddies Ace and Blades. The divers' song filled Sat Control with their Disney chipmunk voices as the dive bell's helium-oxygen mix worked its way out of their vocal cords.

Everyone on Harrier knew they were only getting started.

"They promised," Chase reminded dive control over the radio, as the deputy diving superintendent agonized.

To join divers in the bin for the last few hours of decompression was a custom reserved for mudpuppies—wannabe submariners—a test of initiation supported by generations of aquatic adventurers. Chase had waited years for his father's team to deliver on its promise, and today was his day.

"More paperwork than you're worth if you make a mistake!" The cautious voice of the deputy.

"I won't."

"'Safety first' is the price of admission," the deputy checked with her Captain.

"That one's tough and competent," the Captain remarked.

"He's also fourteen years old."

"Give him a pass. I'll vouch for him."

The bin's intercom erupted again with Fingers' helium-fueled voice competing against the guitar solo. "Chase, remember your chores. Bell checks, dive helmets, hot water suits. Then you can join the party, got it?"

"Copy that, Dad." He suppressed a sigh and began counting the minutes in his head.

Chase descended one last deck, arriving at the moon pool—a black, watery hole, the width of a minivan, passing directly through the ship's hull into the angry sea below. Two circular diving bells suspended above the deceptively still licorice water. The spheres served as elevators to the seabed, permitting safe passage for the brave commuters from the bin, through the black pool to the abyss below. The bells resembled prickly fruit. Bristling with pipework and levers set in precise positions, they dripped with danger tags. Colorful reels hung above the bells, oozing hoses. Dangling like wild hair, they fed the spheres with life-blood helium for breathing, electricity for tooling, and hot water for the dive suits. Finally, the crate no one wanted to use, but everyone knew was there— the bail-out basket. It contained equipment more valuable than any treasure and its maintenance was the difference between life and death.

Chase's role as bell checker was more than mission critical. It was an honor bestowed on a fellow diver, a brother.

This was no ordinary day. This was *the* day. Only the testing stood between Chase and his dream of entering the bin. A methodical puzzle-buster from an early age, nothing could catch him out when he'd set his heart on something.

He inspected each lever carefully and checked off each valve's live-die position against his clipboard. He moved to the basket of last resort, exhaling slowly, controlling his heart rate, and read the gauges on the emergency breathing bottles.

"Empty. Gotcha!" He shouted triumphantly to the camera.

The first of the go-no-go tests was complete. Fail any of them and he would kiss his ambition of joining the dive team goodbye.

Chase was in touching distance of his dream. His attention shifted to the *Kirby Morgan* dive helmets. He placed them one at a time on the moon pool's inspection bench, tackling the hat marked *Fingers* first.

"Too easy," he addressed Harrier's observation cameras.

He checked all three helmets inside and flagged two for routine maintenance, citing worn seals and condemning Ace's for a full refurbishment. He tutted at the cracked face port and scoffed at the apology *Oh Snap* crayoned on the inside.

"I'm gonna re-check," he said, knowing they were watching his every move.

And there it was in Fingers' helmet, a note hidden behind the head cushion: *Condemn mine too. Faulty intercom.*

Chase tackled the hot water suits next, hauling them out of the freshwater rinse tank. The heavy neoprene material was defaced with the diver's name to ensure they didn't get mixed up. He winced at Blade's crudely adapted suit—his trademark—arms and legs sliced short using his legendary Navy Seal knife. He inspected the others.

"Bingo!" The rubber tubes used to pipe hot water around the body panels had been gashed to allow it to cascade out, heating them when working in the otherwise freezing conditions. Chase condemned Blades' suit and flagged the others for refurbishment.

It was the small routine things that killed you in the deep sea diving business: air, comms, and cold.

Chase confirmed with dive control that all checks were complete before demanding his prize. He could hear the captain's voice lecturing folks on their responsibilities before he granted permission.

"Mariner, you are good to go," Dive control announced.

Chase raced to saturation control and entered dive chamber two.

"Standby to be blown down to depth. Remember to equalize, hold your nose and blow your ears, unless you want to implode," reminded Sat Con, taking no chances with the adolescent.

"You have three hours total in the bin, make them count," the anxious female voice confirmed from dive control.

Chase exaggerated the diver's sign for okay to the camera and entered the airlock, ratcheting the hatch closed. He held his mouth and nose and puffed hard into his cheeks to equalize the pressure. The sound of helium mix swirled around him as he waited patiently on the cold steel bench for the GO indicator to turn green.

"Here I come," he shouted over the bin's intercom, grinning at the sound of his high-pitched helium voice, and punching the air as the buzzer confirmed balanced pressure.

He cranked the circular metal door and slowly entered the bin, savoring his first footsteps in the steel chamber, the moment he'd waited for all his life.

His eyes deceived him at the sight: three painted men—one red and two blue—wrestled over a single can of soda, a bag of popcorn, and a remote held aloft like a dagger. The blue figure spoke first. "Son, take a seat, maybe you can settle this. Avatar or Star Wars?"

No sooner was the decision made, the emergency lights flashed and the fire alarm wailed.

38 Rip and Tear

Hershey spun in his chair and switched to channel one, ticked at having to bomb out Season 10 to investigate the source of Harrier's fire alarm. He hailed the deck boss who was known only as Teflon.

"Deep sea diving is neither safe nor easy," yelled the Vietnam vet defensively at the radio op, raging more at himself than the spreading fire. "Son, I've forgotten more than you'll ever learn about this industry."

What Teflon didn't know about Harrier's deck operation wasn't worth knowing. His specialties were too numerous to mention, save two: cutting and explosives. He was the kind of guy you wanted on your side. If something was on fire, he'd know where, why, and who, as surely as if he'd started it himself. Which he never did. Hence his nickname.

"Teflon, old timer, you smell that?" Hershey started over.

The master of understatement prepared his story. Four fires raged, reigniting as soon as they were extinguished. "I hear ya, Hershey. Listen up, we've got a small grease fire underneath the helideck. We're just about to lift it off—only way to get the new winches into the forecastle deck below. Y'all need to be patient. Chopper's not due for another three hours. We're gonna need every minute, son." he yelled over the beating of hot and cold steel.

"Correction, Teflon. The plan's changed. Bird's due in thirty minutes. VIPs aboard too," Hershey announced.

"Goddammit. How long have you known?"

"Seconds," Hershey lied. "Gets worse. The chopper's dry. We need to mobilize the refueling crew."

Teflon glared up at the radio room. "I got two welders underneath, another two cutting above, the forward crane's taking the full weight and there are fires at my ankles, and you want fuel up there?"

The deck boss never failed to deliver but it was going to be tight even for him.

Teflon yelled as he doused the last of the flames. "Hershey, get the night shift out of their beds. Scratch that, they'll already be at their muster stations. Anyways, kill that alarm. It's nothing but a sissy campfire."

Hershey was as relieved as the four divers scrambling into the hyperbaric lifeboat when the warbling stopped. He was now free to feed his addiction with the sound of gunfire from Season 10.

Harrier pitched and rolled as the worsening sea pounded her hull. The vessel's dynamic positioning system groaned as the thrusters worked overtime, struggling to keep her steady in the forty foot waves.

Teflon lit the ship up like a Christmas tree from bow to stern, pushing the day crew hard and the fresh night crew harder still.

Four acetylene track cutters raced each other, spewing rooster tails of fire as they cut a perfect thirty foot square out of the helideck. The tension in the forward crane lines argued with the last inches of uncut steel as the deck hung over the welders by a metallic thread.

The plume of grey smoke confirmed the mighty mid-ship's crane had fired up, snatching both anchors in one grab. The steel swung like a wrecking ball across the deck, wrenching its guide ropes from the hands of the teeth-clenched deck crew.

"Heads up!" somebody shouted, as if their life depended on it. Probably Teflon.

"Snap!" Four welders yelled in unison, diving for cover as the forward crane pulled prematurely, ripping the helipad free. The deck burned brightly, swinging violently from port to starboard, demolishing handrails in the swell.

"That'll be coming out of your wages!" Tefon blared to the crane op.

The cranes changed partners like wild Latin dancers. The forward crane swung aft as the midsection crane arced forward, lowering the new winches through the glowing opening. Smoke billowed, paint smoldered, and the deck gaped open. The Captain covered his eyes. In the space of minutes, Harrier resembled a casualty of war.

The winches clattered against the steel hull, landing in the hole that was the helideck as Harrier plowed through a giant wave.

"Rip and tear!" Teflon yelled.

The insane tango continued as the forward crane returned the stolen deck. The steel was set upon by welders, sending Catherine wheels of sparks high into the night sky.

Teflon checked his watch and turned to his men. "Bird's ETA is fifteen minutes. Fire crews, make your way forward. Stand by to cool the steel above and below with the deck hoses. And tell me days like this don't make you feel alive!"

39 Bird

"Harrier, this is Milkround one. We have you in our sights, approaching on fumes, ETA twelve minutes, do you copy? Over."

"For the love—" Hershey abandoned Season 10, forced to study the radar and perform a basic speed-distance-time calculation, an hour late.

Hershey's addiction to gaming would get someone killed one day, according to Fingers. But he kept the ship running and was the brains behind the salvage hunter's secret weapon—*Chirp*—so he stayed.

"Milkround, I hear you loud and clear. Reduce speed to fifty knots, conserve fuel for approach, and hover."

"Copy that, Harrier. Listen, we can see sparks flying off your bow. Is everything okay for approach?"

The pilot stowed his aviator glasses, the sun long since down. Staring at the NASA intern, he tapped his microphone. "You want on that crate? You'd be safer on a pirate ship, sonny."

The intern nodded nervously.

"Never been better, Milkround," Hershey replied, relying on rock music to mask the sound of the grinders. "Housekeeping's taking a little longer than expected. Maintain approach. Land only when you see the helideck lights illuminated. Over."

The pilots exchanged glances before the chief dipped the nose of the chopper for effect and addressed his VIPs. "Gentlemen, if you look out the cockpit window, you'll notice our destination appears to be on fire. Our ETA is ten minutes. We have fuel for fifteen. Prepare to ditch. Secure your harness, hoods up, adopt the brace position when I instruct you to do so. Nod if you understand."

The two orange-suited passengers complied, one vigorously.

A third of Teflon's deck crew was welding, a third extinguishing fires below, while the rest cooled the helideck with hoses from above. Captain Voss brought the ship around.

"Harrier, this is Milkround. Five hundred feet off your starboard bow. Seven minutes of fuel before we—" The pilot's voice was interrupted by the low-fuel alarm. "Correction Harrier, five minutes of fuel remaining. I can see your landing lights glowing. Over."

"Negative Milkround, those are not landing lights. Approach, hover, and land only when the deck lights are strobing. Over," Hershey urged.

"Copy that, Harrier." The pilot addressed his passengers calmly. "Gentlemen, adopt the brace position. Prepare for sea ditching. Trust your training," he said, as he removed his headset.

The deck boss saw it first. "Incoming!" He shouted to his men, as the rogue wave pounded Harrier's starboard side. The chopper veered away. The hot welds on the helideck steamed like a sauna in the aftermath.

"Where are my strobe lights?" Teflon yelled at his bedraggled crew. He rolled left then right, spying the hook-up cable lolling on the deck. He lunged, making the connection and wincing as the hot steel singed his coveralls. He scrambled to the side as the helipad lit up, clinging to the anti-fall netting, relieved to be off the scorched metal.

The deck crew peeked out from their covered positions as the chopper bounce-landed. Bent double, as much against the wind as the spinning rotors, they advanced on the helicopter, communicating with hand signs to lash it down. They hurled chucks at the wheels, ignoring the smell of burning rubber, and attached a safety line to the fuselage. The thump on the passenger door indicated it was safe to disembark.

The chief pilot exited first, offering his hand out to the deck boss, still lying in the netting. "Cutting it fine?"

Teflon winced at the irony. "Always gotta make an entrance, Bird."

"I called it in two hours ago?" Bird hollered, helping the groaning man to his feet.

"I swear you landed twice."

"I was expecting lights. And not such a hot landing." Bird knelt to investigate the steaming deck.

"I'm getting too old for this crap," Teflon complained, leaning forward to avoid the wilting blades.

"One veteran to another," agreed his old friend.

"Promise me you got my *Cinnabons*, else y'all can hightail it outta here."

"Be delighted. Just as soon as you fuel her up," Bird said, shaking his head.

NASA's chief gaming intern staggered out of the world's most uncomfortable aircraft. Sing gripped the guideline, edged sideways like a crab, and made to stretch.

Teflon yelled at the boy with the NASA backpack, jabbing at the idling red and white blades. "Keep your head down sonny, unless you want to lose it. Follow the green line down two decks to arrivals. Speed it up, else your sneakers will melt." He turned to Bird. "Captain's gonna love him. NASA? He's not old enough to vote."

Next out of the chopper was the naval historian, a serious-looking man in his fifties. He held his own kit bags, required no instruction, stooped, and followed the guideline.

"Who's the officer?" Teflon asked.

Bird moved towards the green line. "Some naval historian. Big cheese. We winched him off a navy sub en route. Norwegian. Goes by the name of Fin Gal. Didn't say a word on the way out."

"Looks like you need a new co-pilot," Teflon said, smirking and pointing at the figure in the cockpit gagging into a paper bag.

"Copy that, old timer. Third one this year," Bird replied, slapping Teflon playfully on the back. "You were the best wingman I ever had. Don't suppose—"

"One word, two letters," Teflon said, cutting him off.

40 The Bin

Sing forced the bulkhead door against the wind and found himself alone in the helicopter reception. He kicked off his singed sneakers and began his escape from the orange survival suit that had strangled him for the last twelve hours. He yanked on the zipper, pulling the watertight neck seal over his head, catching his long hair painfully in the fastener. Sing bowed absurdly as Fin Gal strode into the hallway, demanding to be taken to his quarters immediately.

The boy from NASA was still wrestling comically in his suit.

"Let me help you with that, buddy," Hershey offered, just as Sing snared a second clump of hair in the zipper. "The best thing to do in situations like this is to cut, by which I don't mean the suit." Hershey grabbed scissors from behind the reception and released Sing after several painful clips. The intern was now free to reveal his Season 10 t-shirt, complete with NASA's meatball logo.

Hershey's eyes widened with envy. "Bro, love the camouflage. Does it come in 3XL? How come you got it early? Season 10's been under wraps." Hershey held a clump of hair and extended his free hand. "Friends call me Hershey."

"Name's Sing." The intern gladly accepted the fist bump. "Thanks for the haircut. Ten's out today. My team designed Season 9."

Hershey's eyes spiraled. "Gaming is good," he said, testing the stranger, repeating the gaming mantra.

"I'm the head of Mission-X programming for NASA. Nothing to do with Groundswell or GameMaster," Sing replied defensively, pointing at Hershey's Season 9 cap, offering the environmentalist's right-handed, three-finger salute. "Long story."

Hershey dropped to his knees in mock adoration.

"Gaming is good," the radio operator repeated in awe.

"In moderation," Sing replied, ending Hershey's hero-worshiping.

"Huh?" The large man jumped to his feet with a mixture of disappointment and confusion on his face.

"One hour sessions, max," Sing said firmly. "Playing or programming. No exceptions. Break every hour. Excess breeds mistakes. And mistakes—"

"Mistakes cost lives." Hershey quoted Season 10's catchphrase. Tucking his Atari T-shirt over his full stomach, he chewed on his own words.

"Self-regulation is the key," Sing said, studying the serial gamer blocking the corridor.

"We're all moderates on this ship," Hershey lied as he prepared to bombard the programmer with a thousand tactical questions.

Sing beat Hershey to the point. "The fate of NASA's human space flight depends on a kid who lives on this boat. Chase Hudson."

"Mariner," Hershey corrected him, grinning.

Sing offered up a wedge of official documentation emblazoned with NASA insignia. "All the relevant paperwork's right here, for parental consideration. He needs to accompany me back to Houston Texas immediately to make astronaut selection on Friday morning."

Hershey snatched the wedge of paper and absorbed the revelation. He sat cross-legged, flicking through the files before fanning himself with it. "Good luck with this. NASA saving the world and all that I get. But Season 9? No way, man. Must be a wind-up?" Hershey returned the documents, eyeing the Asian programmer with suspicion.

Sing played the Game card again. "If you help me reach out to Chase—Mariner—I'll guarantee you a unique character skin, a weapon of your design, invisibility cheats, custom sprays, and season upgrades. For life."

It was Hershey's turn to sweat. "And a 3XL Season 10 T-shirt?" He chanced.

"That and a private tour of NASA's Building 9 programming tank in the underworld."

"Sold." Hershey sprang to his feet. "Follow me. Walk and talk. There are a few details you need to know about the family before any sit-down with Fingers."

"Who?"

"Page fifteen in your documentation, paragraph two. Chase's dad," Hershey said wryly. "Oh, and don't ever let the captain hear you call his ship a boat."

Hershey briefed the man from NASA while descending the five flights of stairs to saturation control, sweating as much from excitement as lack of exercise. Sing considered the prospects of mission failure upon arrival, having learned only a fraction of the family's history.

The blood drained from the intern's face as he recognized the dive chamber from NASA's neutral buoyancy laboratory. He gawked at the bewildering factory of cylinders, compressors, and metal pipework filling the heart of the ship, his eyes darting from the chamber to his watch. "Tell me he's not in there."

Hershey smiled. "It's not as bad as it looks. You'll get the whole dysfunctional family at once: Chase, Fingers, Ace and Blades."

Sing didn't answer. He was distracted by a strange throbbing sound. It wasn't the noise of pipework under pressure, or the smell of diesel intensified by the inescapable heat that phased him. He was familiar with dangerous industrial environments. This place was different. The dive chamber called, emitting a strange booming like a heartbeat from within. He processed the scene, identifying the depth meters, and attempted the math. The target depth gauge showed a hundred and eighty feet. Sing groaned.

Hershey tapped the US Navy dive table. "Decompression ascent rates. Four feet per hour."

"Forty-five hours left," Sing's shoulders dropped. "There's no way I can get him to the interview on time now."

Hershey shook his head and tapped the current depth gauge showing twelve feet. The countdown timer flashed three hours. He grabbed the dive chamber intercom and interrupted the booming sound.

Sing massaged his brow. Having narrowly averted mission failure, he rehearsed his script, oblivious to the exchange.

"They're ready," Hershey said hesitantly.

There were four signs of life within the chamber, one blue face, one red, one pink blowing raspberries, and two red cheeks of the wrong sort pressed against the glass. Sing's mind emptied. Any tough conversation was doomed, going by the show of adolescent behavior.

Hershey pointed at Sing's T-shirt with both hands and grinned for the benefit of the painted faces. "You're dealing with a crew of shore-bound saturation divers. You need to be patient. The pink one's the kid you need. Watch the blue one—his dad. He bites."

Sixty seconds passed before Sing received eye contact, the ass was covered, and the booming music stopped.

Each porthole filled with wild eyes, glaring back at the young man from NASA. Bruce Springsteen returned, even louder. *Born in the USA* blared over the external speaker, its chorus sung by the chamber's occupants. The music ended abruptly, leaving the red faces of Ace and Blades disappointed, Chase's pink face staring, and the blue bearded face of Fingers Hudson doing the talking.

"So, outer space meets inner space. State your business, Mr NASA, in as few words as possible."

Sing's mouth opened, but his words stalled, the intern shocked at the high-pitched voice coming from the soldier's face.

Hershey rescued him. "This guy," tapping Sing on the shoulder, "is the programmer behind *GameMaster's* Season 9. He works for NASA, who need Chase to go into space to save the world. Or was it their reputation? Anyway, you should hear him out."

All four faces disappeared, returning moments later from different portholes, two holding pens, one wincing. It was the turn of Blades—the red scarred face—to speak. "Season 9 was totaled last Friday by a squad of environmentalists."

"Called themselves *Groundswell*," Ace interrupted, finishing Blade's sentence. "Those high-rollers rejected a nine million dollar prize just to stick it to you, *GameMaster*—NASA, whoever the hell y'all are."

"Gaming is good," yelled Blades, slapping Ace roughly on the back.

Chase's face drained before he dropped out of sight.

Sing realized he was swimming in the company of sharks, so he raised the stakes. "It wasn't *GameMaster* behind Season 9. It was us, NASA. And one of the high-rolling environmentalists is in your chamber." He swallowed as he watched the three remaining faces vanish.

41 Aqua

"No point staying here, bro," Hershey said as he blew down the paperwork in the airlock, rubbing his stomach. "Safest place for us is the captain's map room. An orderly retreat is required I fear, via the galley."

Hershey had to avoid as many people on the ship as NASA, after creating the helicopter landing emergency. He checked the corridor, walked and talked. "Remaining decompression time is two hours, forty-five minutes. Then they release the animals. Our deal's still good, right?"

Sing nodded, following Hershey's heels in a trance, deaf to his barrage of Season 10 questions. NASA's mission was unraveling with every step.

Harrier heaved from port to starboard, turning the simple task of walking into a game of human pinball. Sing ascended the flights of stairs, bouncing painfully against the walls decorated in tributes to the treasure hunters, but mostly to one man—Fingers Hudson.

Hershey held fast with the ease of a seasoned mariner as the ship's bow hit the trough of a wave sending Sing sprawling into the galley. His cries of embarrassment were drowned by jeering and the drumming of silverware against tables.

Hershey helped his fast friend to his feet. "News travels fast onboard. Play the *GameMaster* card. Trust me. Most of the crew are serial gamers."

Sing groaned, as much from motion sickness as from the admission.

"Teflon's gunning for you," somebody shouted from the kitchen.

"Bird, too." Another helpful voice.

"Gotta run, bro, DP's failing. The ship's rock and roll," Hershey made a wave motion with his hand.

Sing looked blankly at the jovial man.

"DP, Dynamic positioning. The ship's stabilization system. Or lack of it," Hershey explained hurriedly, looking over his shoulder. "Don't worry, it happens all the time on the old gal. It's a killer when the divers are on bottom or during helicopter take-off and landing. But let's face it, no one's going anywhere for now." Hershey headed to the corridor.

The one thing the nano-electronics wizard liked more than gaming was food, and Hershey never skipped a meal. He strode brazenly to the canteen hatch and addressed the queue of hungry seamen. "Gaming is good." The line saluted back. He grabbed a burger and offered some final advice to NASA. "Bro, whatever you do next, don't touch the kit in the map room."

Sing sloped towards the end of the line, his mission floundering worse than the ship.

"*Signor*, what's with the long face? Come try Coolio's famous apple pie festooned with Italian ice cream," the camp boss beckoned. "I take it personally if you no accept. *Capiche*?"

Sing nodded, moving awkwardly to the front of the queue, keeping his center of gravity as low as possible. "Now, NASA, you go and sit with Aqua Marina over there, away from this riff-raff. Bella beautiful is Chase's tutor, and the best damn ROV submarine pilot in the business, no?" Coolio pointed vigorously at the woman sitting in the corner. The queue jeered, feigning jealousy. The Italian handed over the steaming bowl of American Dream, gesturing insistently with his serving spoon, attempting to calm the noisy line.

Marina silenced the room and Coolio with a single disapproving look.

"*Grazi*," Sing thanked Coolio, grasping the bowl laden with steaming pie and swirls of ice cream; he headed for Chase's tutor.

"*Prego*," Coolio replied, watching the intern stumble in the pitch and roll and collide with Marina's table.

Her almond eyes hinted at a smile. "New to this?" She asked as he wiped the cream from his face and nodded.

In his peripheral vision, he noted the Norwegian from the flight sitting with his back to the others, avoiding eye contact.

"Yes, ma'am," Sing answered. His appetite waned as the motion worsened.

"So, you're NASA," Marina whispered sarcastically, as if the crew were listening, which they were.

Sing nodded in slow motion, staring at the pie.

"Well, listen up NASA, as I don't do conspiracy theory. Nor am I much of a conversationalist. But if you're here to reprimand Chase for any of his environmental stunts, you'll have a long swim home."

The silence was interrupted as Harrier's bow slammed through the waves, the sound of gaming chatter building behind them. Marina continued. "Hershey's a surprisingly good judge of character. He seems to like you, which is the only reason we're having this conversation."

Sing found the courage to speak. "Reprimand? On the contrary," he remembered his script and placed the official-looking file marked *Mariner* on the table, forcing Marina's defined eyebrows to rise suspiciously. "NASA wants to invest in Chase's unique set of skills. It sounds like you and Hershey are to thank for that. We—NASA, Mission-X—want to give him a shot at the junior astronaut program. And a full academic bursary irrespective of the outcome." He studied the ROV pilot for a reaction; receiving none, he continued. "You think that's a mistake?"

Marina ignored his question and searched his face. "Why, Chase?"

Sing placed a USB stick next to the manila file, unable to hide his swallow. "NASA needs his help. It's all on here."

None of this made any sense to anyone, least of all the crew of Harrier. But the central truth was the NASA brand. Captain Voss had allowed the agency to land on his ship. If it was good enough for him, it was good enough for them.

Aqua Marina rescued the thumb drive as it skittered across the table, studying it as if it were a glass of fine wine. Sing could see she had made the connection, spotting the opportunity for the boy.

"He's the smartest kid I've ever tutored," she said, flicking through the manila file. "But he hates studying and lives in the shadow of his father. He's always trying to prove himself. It's criminal. I blame the military boarding school when Fingers was on active duty. But don't be too quick to judge his dad for that—raising a kid on your own's tough, and virtually impossible in the service. Chase is passionate to the extreme. Give him a puzzle, and he's off. Fiercely loyal too. Gets that from his father. If he could only start believing in himself."

"There is a way," Sing said, sounding energized. "Mission-X would build his confidence, and he'd be on the program with his two best friends?"

"As long as it's not Ace and Blades," she replied, standing. "His real *besties* are virtual. Inseparable. Quite normal for his generation I guess. NASA's academic reputation will only get you so far on this tub, buddy. You're going to have to convince Fingers and his team first. So, good luck there."

"Marina," Sing blurted out, as she made for the door. "Get a message to Chase, please. Tell him I can help with the *Riddle of the Viking.*"

She gestured to the kitchen hatch, pocketed the thumb drive, and winked. "Plates over there when you've finished. I recommend you hide in the captain's map room. The guys get out in a couple of hours. Nice meeting you, kid."

42 Red Legend

Boatless man is tied to the land.
Båtlaus mann er bunden til land.

Sing jolted upright as the galley's shutters slammed closed. His mission was far from click and collect. It was clear that the intern had to get ahead of the game he found himself playing—or face failure. He followed Marina's advice.

He scoured the corridors searching for the map room. Every floor and door appeared the same. The higher he got, the worse he felt with the ship's motion. He searched for fresh air, only to find the stern-facing portholes fixed. His breath fogged the glass as his eyes darted towards a burst of fire on the aft deck. The steel screamed as grinders beveled sparks and welders beaded hot molten seams on iron. Two cranes, one huge, the other shaped like a monster's claw, worked in concert. Their engines whined and hooks swung as their operators hastily arranged deep sea diving equipment with pinpoint accuracy on the packed decks.

Sing had seen the machines before. NASA's Neutral Buoyancy Lab used the Remotely Operated Vehicles—ROVs—in the world's largest pool, to simulate construction in space. He watched as the fluorescent mini-subs were stacked high. Like weird beasts caged in a zoo, their claws extended through the bars as if trying to escape. The scene confirmed that this was no ordinary ship, and he was on no regular mission.

He turned, steadying himself against a steel-plated oval door, anonymous but for a small sign marked *Private, Authorized Personnel Only.*

He knocked, preparing to ask for forgiveness, as the ship pitched hard to port, launching him into the room. The door slammed behind him as *Harrier* heaved to starboard. His hands reached out, feeling the underside of a wooden table and the smell of musty oak. Sing picked himself up, his eyes adjusting with the help of the light eking under the drawn blinds.

In the dull light, he could make out plaques and maps covering every inch of wall. One stood out—twice the size of the others—*Båtlaus mann er bunden til land*. Boatless man is tied to the land. A feast of maritime instruments weighed down exotic charts and threadbare scrolls. Strings and pins radiated from a central flag marked *Red Legend*.

There was no mistaking the room's importance. Oozing with history, it was a place of planning. And secrets.

Sing had gleaned enough from the professor's notes on Chase to hint that NASA could help the boy with his riddle. But the research in the map room was on a different scale.

Sing couldn't have known that Captain Voss and Chase shared the same dream for different reasons. *Red Legend* was the opportunity for the Captain and all Americans to prove their Viking ancestry by finding the mythical ships of Erik the Red. Chase's dream was to prove the very opposite: No ships, no legend, no link for Runa Erikson to the most fearsome Viking of all. Rubbish the legend and rubbish the rumors that caused the hurt and robbed her of sleep.

Nor did Sing understand the significance of the book that lay open on the oak table—the *Orcadian Sagas*, chronicling Scottish history under Viking rule. It was a record of done deeds, scribed by the men of Orkney a thousand years ago. They claimed the Viking marauder had conquered then colonized the Americas, but their quest to return to Norway with proof had failed, with his ship last seen beached in Scotland on the rocks at Bruich.

Sing reached for the shaft of light coming from the window, uncomfortable with his intrusion. The blind recoiled at his touch, forcing him to shield his eyes as the map room flooded with light from Harrier's midships.

Exhausted and seasick, he slumped into the nearest chair.

He surveyed the ship's table, noticing one of the ancient charts had moved to reveal a device alien to the antiques filling the room. He squinted at the crystal white gadget the size of a hockey puck and leaned towards it. Two sticky notes were attached to it, one yellow, the other red. *Chirp,* scribbled on the yellow. *Don't touch. LOL Mariner & Hershey,* on the other.

"Play popular music," Sing commanded. He reclined optimistically as the gadget's circular edge shone blue, rotated slowly clockwise, then faded. He leaned forward, a quizzical look formed on his face. "*Chirp,* play popular music." The rim pulsed yellow then faded. "*Chirp,* play something, anything."

"Unauthorized voice pattern," the device warned, throbbing red, rotating anti-clockwise, humming through the table. The bass vibration intensified. Sing covered his ears against the noise as it peaked then vanished like a wisp of smoke.

"Well, that was an anti—" He inhaled his words as a sonic boom blew him out of the captain's chair, shattering the stern-facing observation window.

Sing lay on the floor and took the seconds he needed to audit his injuries. It was as if the device had stung him. His shock-infused state played tricks on his eyes as the Big Dipper stared back down at him from the ceiling, the North Star circled on the celestial map.

A ghostly silhouette holding an oil lamp revealed itself in the doorway. The uniformed man strode towards him, yanking the blind down over the shattered window, pointing at the red warning note stating 'don't touch' still somehow attached to *Chirp*. He turned abruptly, adjusted his Captain's hat, and left the way he'd arrived, unimpressed.

Sing took a last curious look at the star constellation before finding the strength to move. He righted the chair, pushed himself up, and fought the desire to sleep on his feet as he assessed the damage he'd caused. He tidied the strewn charts and straightened the pictures, then froze at the sound of shouting. He lunged at the bulkhead but grabbed at the blind, ripping it free as the boom from a wave hit.

He looked out. There she was. Aqua Marina stood on the aft deck, directing the midships crane. Sing watched in horror as a second giant wave broke over the starboard rail, spewing sea spray high into the air, obscuring everything.

He pressed his face as close to the shattered glass as he dared. Marina spied him, making the Groundswell salute as the water receded around her. He collapsed into the captain's chair for a second time, as embarrassed as he was exhausted, surrendering to fatigue in the safest room on the ship.

The dive crew stirred deep in the belly of the beast, as the explosive vibration traveled through the ship's hull, interrupting the movie.

"NASA found *Chirp* then," Ace remarked to Blades, winking at Chase.

"Gonna need to replace the glass again," the double act continued.

"Least we know where he is," Fingers remarked, shooshing them, returning to his favorite film.

43 Avatar

Lizard-like aliens encircled Sing; wild savages, they spoke in a strange tongue while a beautiful mermaid whispered his name. And in that instant he realized he was awake.

"NASA!" Marina shouted, leaning over him. The panel of six stared—two red faces, one blue, one pink, the mermaid, and a familiar man in uniform.

Sing wiped the sleep from his eyes, now the size of headlamps, as the parlay began.

"I believe you've already met Captain Voss," Fingers jabbed his thumb in the direction of the impeccably dressed man with a kind face and white cropped beard. He waived Sing's paperwork as he addressed the room, his voice still pitchy as the helium worked its way out of his system. "Here's what we know. NASA needs to secure a team of tough, competent teenagers. Chase and his adolescent buddies measure up nicely. According to your file, you've already tested them virtually to destruction for months. Now you need to profile them physically, am I right?"

Fingers had learned of the Groundswell environmental movement less than three hours beforehand. He doubted its childish motives as much as NASA's intention to ever pay the prize money.

Sing nodded as Fingers' voice began to sound more human, despite his blue face. "These papers say you need my son for a week for a try-out on NASA's Mission-X junior astronaut selection program in Houston, leaving tonight?" Fingers paused, assessing his team's body language.

Three of them sat with arms tightly folded. Blades polished his knife and Ace picked his nose as Chase leaned forward, his eyes shifting from Marina to Sing.

Sing padded his offer. "We're offering two tickets."

"Your timing sucks, NASA." Fingers shot the offer down in flight with an arrow of truth. "Harrier is about to embark on the most significant archaeological dive of the century. *Red Legend.* We can't spare a soul, even Chase."

"Especially Chase," Marina added.

Sing back-peddled, perspiring. "I'll be chaperoning him at all times,"

Marina glanced at the shattered window and saluted his handy work.

Fingers pointed roughly at Ace and Blades. "According to these two, NASA killed the winners of Season 9 during the last simulated mission and kept the nine million dollar prize?"

We'll have Chase home in less than a week, in good time for Christmas." Sing was losing the skirmish, the battle, and the entire war, in one sitting.

"So, here's how this is going to play out," Fingers announced after an engineered silence. He ignored his son's waving arm, a habit that had not gone unnoticed over the years. "Assuming the boy wants to go, we have certain demands over and above your academic offer. Captain Voss wants the right to salvage any NASA equipment left on the seabed since 1965. We want to borrow the space station's prototype Canada Arm, the titanium crane reportedly at the Neutral Buoyancy Lab in Texas. And Ace and Blades want one of the new Starliner Astrosuits. Each."

Fingers paused, looking directly into Sing's eyes. "*I* want nothing more than the safe return of my son. Failure to do so will result in your slow and painful death." He slammed his fist on the desk, sending a stack of manuscripts flying. Blade's dive knife sank into the table in agreement. "How say you, NASA?"

Chase raised his hand again and took a deep breath. "Before you adults wrap up on my behalf, I have one demand. Well, two. Firstly, no exams."

Marina rolled her eyes.

Sing nodded.

"And help with the other thing you promised, The Riddle of the Viking. You can explain how NASA knows about this some other time." His eyes darted from Marina to Sing.

Chase's obsession was to uncover the hidden meaning behind Groundswell's playbook. Runa was concealing something in its wisdom, of that he was convinced.

Sing clapped. "I can make this work, but we have to be in Houston in twenty-four hours."

Fingers exchanged a curious look with Marina before he stood. "One last thing."

Sing slumped back down.

"Why's NASA continued with the astronaut program when the World Health Organization has condemned all human space travel?" He pointed to the headline on the captain's *Washington Post.*

"They're wrong, and we can prove it, but we need to get in the air now." Sing made to leave.

The map room's door swung open in slow motion revealing Hershey's ear, his usually smiling face frowning. "Guys, we have a problem."

"Forgotten your password for Season 9?" Ace scoffed.

"Bird found you then?" Blades asked, smirking.

Hershey's voice was devoid of humor. "The chopper's going nowhere thanks to Teflon's welders. We've got six flats and only one spare."

44 Runflat

"Weather's up, choppers down." Fingers removed the knife from the captain's table and addressed the team. His blue face was comically serious as he motioned toward his son and the boy from NASA. "Yet we need to get these two fellas three hundred miles to the US mainland by tomorrow. Ideas? And there's no such thing as a stupid question."

"Fifteen hundred miles to Houston in twenty-four hours." Sing's voice broke the silence.

"Sixteen hundred," corrected the captain, his eyes fixed on the flag in the center of the table. Voss was all for helping the space agency, but heading in the wrong direction when operation Red Legend beckoned wasn't going to happen, no matter what they offered.

Sing withdrew, unable to contribute to the crazy ideas as they rolled in.

"All things considered, we're looking at a delay of twenty-four to forty-eight hours, subject to availability, parts, weather window, and a brave pilot," Hershey conceded, heading back out.

Fingers glanced at the captain, seeking approval, ignoring his son's hand in the air for the second time.

"It won't work," Sing said, as he stared through his hands, his mission crumbling. "NASA forfeits to the military squad if we're late. The interview's competitive. The deadline's fixed by a guy intent on crushing the agency's future as we know it."

"Competitive?" Chase exclaimed, his hand recoiling.

"You needn't worry," the intern's voice was resigned to failure. "Your team was always our team. But the wider agency was hellbent on considering additional military candidates."

Friday's dawn deadline was an engineered impossibility. NASA's Director One had seen to that.

Sing noticed it again—the glint in Chase's eye—a secret. He played his final card, the bluff. "NASA's already secured the commitment of your leader, Runa Erikson. We've got a guy at the North Pole as we speak."

"Red Jacket." Chase made the connection instantly, checking his watch. "Your guy is currently a prisoner in Runa's airlock," he said, grinning.

"Fox Washington?" Sing's face showed confusion and alarm.

"Run Flat, that's our solution for the chopper," Chase said cryptically.

Blades did all the talking after a reluctant silence. "We planted *Chirp* on a Norwegian ship last month in port. Well, Mariner did. I mean, who would suspect a kid in a dingy?

"Do I want to hear this?" Fingers asked.

"The story ends well, boss. Our old Seal team showed up in town on a joint naval exercise with the Norwegians. *Chirp* messed up their sonar big time. The Norwegians returned, reporting zero kills, eclipsed by our guys."

"And how does that help us take off?" Fingers grip tightened on his seat.

"They clocked him removing the evidence from their hull, and bored a hole in ours, under our waterline."

"Which Mariner filled with miracle foam—Run Flat," Ace added. "That goop will expand and fill anything, anywhere. Hell, we're still floating, aren't we?"

Chase looked at his unsmiling father. "There's a case of it in my locker."

Fingers glared at his men. "You two pin-heads are lucky I didn't find out in the dive bell. Else I'd have cut off your air supply, maybe more. Next time, come through me to get to him.

"The boy needs to start hanging out with kids his age," said Marina..

"All credit to Mariner," Ace muttered. "The kid deserves an Oscar, not a roasting."

"One more word and you're over the side," Fingers looked as dangerous as a blue face could.

Blades winked at Chase.

"None of this leaves the room." Captain Voss pointed to Blade's knife and rubbed his brow. "Fingers, your men owe me a table and hull repair, just as soon as we reach dry land."

"Pull a stunt like that again—" Fingers paused for the longest moment, searching his son's eyes, before banging his fist and giving him the order. "Go get your goop. Raise Teflon on the radio and busy him on the chopper. Find Bird. He's got sixty minutes to refuel. And someone get Hershey off that goddamn game."

45 Highlander

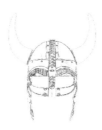

Scott McMurdo had been adventurous from an early age. He considered the lochs and glens of Varrich Estate his playground, swimming in the frigid pools and bouldering on the ancient crags year-round. He'd developed an affinity with the land, living with the gamekeeper, explaining why its protection ran deep in his veins.

Scott paused midway along the stone causeway, separating the picturesque fishing village of Finkle from the Talmine peninsula. He gazed at the whirlpool of crystal white water as it clashed with the ocean blue, the eternal battle between current and tide. His mind swirled with the vortex, wondering if he'd done enough for Runa?

The boy had phoned UNIS from the village phone box, but his plea had been dismissed by the University of Svalbard's rescue center as an adolescent's prank. With the last of his cash, he'd dialed the governor's office and uttered the two magic words: Red Jacket.

With Norwegian efficiency, the emotionless operator routed the teenage caller to someone who cared as deeply for the environment as he did for the victim. The conversation with the governor of Svalbard was cut short by a lack of coins though, leaving Scott cursing his Highland isolation, and Odin Berg mobilizing Runa's rescue squad.

Scott took a last look at the phenomenon of the fast tide versus the full moon, and then studying the horizon, he ran to the dunes.

In contrast to Finkle's multi-colored buildings and ancient granite harbor, Talmine was a feast of white beaches, sand bars, and connected islets. The largest was dotted with the farmer's sheep and was about to be swamped by the unusually high tide.

With the fully waxed moon's gravity busting the tideline, Scott knew he had to act quickly to save the livestock. He could risk crossing the tidal sandbar with its notorious mudflats or run in the opposite direction to his secret rendezvous.

The village elders swore there was nothing the boy couldn't fix. The farmer's barn was an Aladdin's cave of abandoned equipment and now a temple to Scott's mechanical projects, each one grander than the next. His favorite, parked in the long beach grass, was Badger—a series two, short wheel-based Landrover Defender. It was the farmer's favorite and a gamekeeper's go-to for trundling around the moors in any season. Scott had saved the classic off-roader from the scrap heap. All torque and no speed, the machine was perfect for inspecting fences over rough ground, winching flotsam up the sea cliffs, and hauling grateful locals out of snowdrifts—his best earner.

He grabbed Chase's latest version of *Chirp* and switched it from *flee* to *feed,* placing it on Badger's bonnet for maximum resonance.

Inaudible to humans, *Chirp*'s ultrasonic signal blasted the feeding call towards the sheep, ignorant of their peril on the islet. The flock of hungry beasts splashed across the shrinking causeway, stampeding towards the sound in search of the promised meal.

"To the launch pad!" Scott announced to Badger, jumping into the soft sand from the top of its rugged cab.

46 Super Guppy

NASA's Super Guppy aborted its second landing attempt at Inverness airport in the Scottish Highlands. Named after the ugliest fish on the planet, its pilots throttled back to avoid a fresh wave of protestors chaining themselves across the runway.

The iconic heavy-lift aircraft resembled an alien's head on the body of a silver whale and had a habit of attracting attention. Its arrival jammed the local police station's switchboard with reports of extraterrestrial landings, rubber-necking automobile accidents, and trespassing at the airport.

Two swarms of onlookers made for the perimeter fencing. One fought for the best spot to photograph the bizarre craft. The other waved protest banners and cut holes in the chainmail fence.

The Guppy's payload: mobile satellite launch equipment, bound for Mellness, Scotland's first spaceport; and one anxious passenger.

NASA intern Pearl Washington clawed her way out of the jump seat squashed in behind the three pilots. She stretched and yawned, having hitched a seventeen-hour ride on the world's second most uncomfortable aircraft—the worst being Bird's 1998 Sikorsky Superhawk helicopter that had carried Sing to the Harrier dive ship. She followed the pilots eagerly, squeezing into the packed cargo bay. The aircrew covered their ears against the screeching hinges as the head of the Guppy swung open at ninety degrees.

Capable of swallowing two T-38 jets, the ground crew gasped at the sight.

"*Stoater*," the Scottish baggage handler said in awe. "Americans *dinae* pack light."

"*Numpty*," his mate said, "This came *fae ooter* space. I've seen it on the telly."

"Away with the blethering, *ya eejits*," their supervisor complained. "Get the *Big Yin* empty *afore* the greenies return."

Pearl caught the crew staring in her direction. Spoiling them with a wave, she pulled on the collar of her green NASA jacket with pride. Shivering against the December chill, she shouted to the men that were acting like boys. "See y'all in 24hours."

At that very moment, Pearl's twin, Fox Washington in his soon to be notorious red jacket, landed near the North Pole. Sing was somewhere off the US eastern seaboard, which left her with the most straightforward task on the northern tip of Scotland—or Alba, according to the fiercely proud locals.

Pearl shouldered her backpack, reached for her Oakleys, and drew down her baseball cap, as much against the wind as the camera flashes from the perimeter fence. Her every move was captured by the local paparazzi's telephoto lens.

She strode to Arrivals, regretting her agency apparel as the sound of jeering from the banner-waving protestors grew. She jogged as they shook the chainmail fence, chanting *NASA Keep Out*, and *Save Eagle Tree!* She sprinted when a woman approached clenching wire cutters in one hand and paint bombs in the other, swithering between Pearl and the silver whale.

Pearl entered the paint-splattered Arrivals hall at speed, already considering mission failure as she reached the sign saying *Fàilte gu Alba*.

"Welcome to Scotland, my dear," announced a rotund, tartan-clad lady pointing at the sign, beaming the widest smile the intern had ever seen.

Pearl handed her blue eagle passport across the immigration desk.

"Ooh, an American," the kind-faced woman waved the prize above her head, beckoning the attention of a man dozing at the back of the empty Arrivals hall. "Hamish!" Tartan Lady shouted.

The man wearing traditional Scottish dress continued to doze.

"We love Americans in the Highlands, don't we Auld Hamish!" Tartan Lady hollered.

The taxi driver slumbered on.

The glass in Arrivals shook with her next jibe: "Sit up straight else you'll scare the tourists!" And Auld Hamish jolted upright, fixing his kilt.

Tartan Lady perched her reading glasses on the end of her nose, squinting at a list of questions she had read a thousand times. "What's the purpose of your visit to our bonny wee country? How long will you be staying with us? And at what address can we find you at? There we go, my dear, three questions for the price of one." She neither paused for breath nor waited for answers. Stamping Pearl's passport, she chuckled at her own humor, and escorted her VIP through the baggage hall. She pointed at the kilted man in tow. "You'll be using our cousin Auld Hamish then? Old Hamish the taximan? You'll hay to get used to our language and ways if you're to survive the night here, my dear."

The taximan beamed, extending both hands.

"Auld Hamish'll get you passed the protesters, then north. Not to be confused with his brother, Young Hamish, Finkle's Ferryman. Those lovely young men from NASA have arranged it."

"Customs check." A voice barked from the room on the right.

"She's wee me. Away back to your tea," Tartan Lady ordered, returning to greet the paint-splattered pilots racing into immigration.

"I'm heading for the fishing village of Finkle, Varrich Arms Hotel," Pearl announced, stopping Tartan Lady mid-stride.

"I'll make the call," the woman's face transformed with pride, simultaneously gesturing for the pilots to wait.

"Her sister, my wife, runs Finkle's only hotel," Auld Hamish said in a thick Scottish accent.

Pearl returned his warm smile.

"Aye, we're a tight-knit community up north, my dear," the taximan winked, admiring her jacket's NASA meatball logo. "You might want to turn that funcy jacket inside oot, afore we ging ootside."

47 Outsider

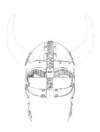

Keen to draw on his local knowledge, Pearl accepted his offer to join him up front, away from the odor of the four-legged and feathered passengers in the back.

Wasting no time, she mentioned NASA's plan to invite one of the village children to attend space camp in Houston. "A fourteen year old boy, by the name of—"

"Scott McMurdo," interrupted the driver, his grin widening.

"How—"

"That one's wise beyond his years. A true Highlander," he continued over the baaing and clucking coming from the back.

Pearl rolled down the window. "Motion sickness," she insisted, listening to the taximan as they weaved their way along the undulating roads, twisting and turning like a rough sea. Her hopes for the mission rose on the crest of Scott's engineering antics and fell with the tales of his environmental follies.

Hamish proudly recounted the day Scott McMurdo achieved folk hero status with 'his' movement, Groundswell. Their activists returned half a million crisp bags to their source manufacturer and the campaign brought *Royal Mail* to its knees.

The taximan paused for a long moment, murmuring. "Does nae seem to matter what the boy does. His da winnae give him a blind bit of attention."

Pearl tried not to look sideways.

"His dad ignores him. Always has." Hamish reverted to the Queen's English. "Away on the oil rigs. Working, working, working."

The vehicle shuddered as a gravel track replaced the road. "The lights of Wick are ahead," the taximan announced, as he pulled into a gas station that boasted a single pump.

Pearl leaned out the window, her face matching the green of her jacket.

Hamish transferred supply boxes to an ancient Landrover abandoned next to the attendant's hut. "We'll finish the journey to Varrich in this old beauty. The roads can get a bit dicey this time of year."

Three new passengers bustled out of the tiny shack: Mrs Mack, the shopkeeper, carrying a large string package; Farmer Dod, the farmer, pulled by his sheepdog; and Scott's uncle, Angus McMurdo, the gamekeeper, a bearded giant dressed in camouflage and carrying a shotgun over his arm.

"How do we all fit in?" Pearl asked, looking at the Landrover and the assortment of livestock.

"Away hame, ya big dafty." Her question answered by the taximan spanking the sheep on the rump, shouting after the beast as it scampered off into its highland pasture.

The final ninety minute leg to Varrich was accompanied by the sheepdog licking the windscreen, nudging the driver faster, and growling at the community radio DJ's taste in music.

"Dinnae be so rude, Auld Hamish," Mrs Mack, Finkle's only shopkeeper, accused Varrich's only taxi driver. "Our American guest cannae understand a word if you're gan ta speak Gaelic all the way. You're nae better, Farmer Dod." She prodded the man sitting next to the driver, tossing chocolate onto his lap, sending his dog Jess wild.

"What brings you this far north?" Mrs Mack asked, eager to secure gossip from the stranger. The Landrover veered onto the verge as the taximan looked over his shoulder, keen to answer the question himself.

"Keep your eyes on the road, Auld Hamish," Mrs Mack protested loudly, "else you'll end us all, ya daft auld git."

"Pearl here's from NASA. They're going to send Scott to the moon," he announced undeterred, looking in the rear view mirror for a reaction.

Farmer Dod coughed, Jess barked, and the keeper stirred from his thoughts. "What are you talking aboot, Auld Hamish? Have ya lost yer mind?" The man was shocked. "What's this aboot ma nephew gan tae space?"

Pearl swallowed at the news she was sitting next to Scott's uncle. "Hi, Pearl Washington from NASA, sir," she offered her hand first to Mrs Mack, then to the gamekeeper. "It's my first time to Scotland, and I'm heading to—"

"This is nae Scotland, lassie. This is the Highlands," corrected the gruff gamekeeper, his huge red beard touching her as he spoke. "Two certainties. My nephew's done nothing wrong. And he's going naywhere."

"Let the girl speak, Angus McMurdo." Mrs Mack was the only person in the village allowed to call the keeper by his real name.

"What ever it was, he was wee me," Farmer Dod remarked, as Jess barked in agreement. "Definitely wee me."

"Scott's in no trouble whatsoever, Mr McMurdo. I'm here to inspect the new spaceport site at Mellness." Pearl backtracked fast to prevent the journey from turning into a disaster, clutching at the white lie. "It's true NASA wants to offer your nephew a week at space camp in Houston, but it's a bit closer to Earth than Auld Hamish might like. Of course, I need to discuss it with Scott's parents."

The passengers all sighed.

"Firstly, naebody calls me Mr McMurdo, lassie."

"He prefers Big Angus." Mrs Mack rescued her with a sympathetic smile. "But most folks call him the keeper, owing to his responsibilities."

"Secondly, Scott's a pretty special lad. I'm his legal guardian, so any talking you'll do wee me. Sure, you're nae from Social Services?"

The driver crunched the gears, and the Landrover's engine whined in neutral.

"What, with an accent like that?" Somebody said from the front.

The keeper turned awkwardly to study her reaction. "He lives with my wife and me at the keeper's cottage on the Varrich Estate. His Dad, my brother Jock, works on the North Sea oil rigs and sends every penny back to the village, afore you start judging! The brains of the family, head of the clan." Angus McMurdo waited for Pearl to react. When she didn't, he looked at her with suspicion. "You're definitely nay a greenie, despite the color of your fancy jacket? What exactly do you want from us?"

"Nothing more than to check on the spaceport and to meet Scott?" Pearl replied, playing the long game.

"Thought you was one of them—the protestors. Dinna get me wrong, our livelihoods depend on us respecting the environment. Isn't that right, Farmer Dod? And I'll have you know I'm a card-carrying member of the boy's movement, Groundswell."

"Me too," chorused the others.

"Tell her," insisted the shopkeeper, tugging the keeper's red beard.

"Those protesters, the greenies, are trying to shut down the Mellness spaceport. The first new industry we've had in these parts for fifty years," the keeper grumbled. "Most of them dinnae even live here. They're flying pickets fae Inverness. Or worse, lowlanders."

Mrs Mack slapped the keeper's knee. "You've spent the whole day filing a petition on behalf of the villagers to move Eagle Tree from the Mellness launch site."

The Eagle Tree. The occasional nesting ground of fickle-winged residents. The birds of prey flitted between it and their favored site at the ruin of Varrich castle.

"What folks forget is that living this far north, we must be resourceful to make a living." The keeper was in no mood for compromise. "Take my brother Jock. Look at the sacrifices he makes. Does nae see his boy for months at a time. And there's young Hamish, his brother, Finkle's ferryman, captain of the Sea Nymph. Oot of work since they built the causeway. Finkle used to be a thriving wee fishing village when I was a lad. Now we're doon to two part-time lobstermen. I blame the European quotas and those greedy Russian industrial trawlers."

"Aye, Angus," Mrs Mack continued "We need the jobs to keep our village community together, nae bleeding eagles. We lose a family to the Lowlands every year. What hope have we for the next generation? Take young Scott. I had the headmistress, Mrs McFearson, in my shop just last week whining about him. 'Naturally talented but lacking focus,' she said. What does she expect with a school population of twelve. And dinnae start me on her son, picking on Scott just for being different, smart-like."

"Weasel," remarked the keeper. "That lad's the second most unpopular person in Varrich so he is. Rotten to the core."

"Top of the list is his Da," Farmer Dod turned to face the keeper. "The copper, Sergeant McFearson. Oot to get the McMurdos at every opportunity. Aye, the father's the one to watch."

"Well poor Pearl's heard quite enough about the village nasties," interrupted Mrs Mack. "Big Angus here has been doing fine work, leading the campaign to fight for the spaceport, trying to relocate those buzzards. And we're proud of him, aren't we, Dod?"

"Aye, we are indeed Mrs Mack, and his nephew," Dod replied, wrestling with Jess on his lap. "If it were nae for Scott's help, I could nae run the farm at my age. The boy never gives up on old things, always fixing."

"Aye, he's a recycler that one. Mr Resourceful," the keeper said proudly. "You want to meet him you say?"

"He'll be over in Talmine Bay with Badger right now," Farmer Dod beamed, "chasing my sheep off the island before the storm hits tonight. The lad takes nothing for his trouble, never has. I've tried as many times. All he wants is to tinker wee stuff in my barn. Like a son to me, that one."

"Look oot!" The keeper shouted as black flashes crossed the single track road.

"Sorry," Hamish yelled, as the Landrover hit a pothole.

"Lights, man!" the keeper ordered. "This is when the beasts come oot."

Pearl glanced left and right.

"The big *yins*. Four hoofs wee antlers," Farmer Dod explained, searching for his glasses.

"NASA, *aye?*" The keeper's voice softened before he launched a salvo of questions. Knowledge, size, frequency of satellite launches—would all be of interest to the thirsty patrons in the *Varrich Arms* at opening time.

Pearl spotted her opportunity to win favor, sharing everything, holding back only the truth behind her mission.

"Best if you meet him on Talmine beach after he's rounded up Dod's sheep," the keeper advised. "But you'll hae to be quick as it's pitch dark by three pm this far north. The boy will be at the Mellness launchpad wee Badger, checking the council's pitiful deer fence. It's nae big enough to keep the big reds oot, so he'll be chasing them aff wee that Chirp gadget. The taximan'll run you over the causeway once you've settled in. Won't you, Auld Hamish? And he winnae be charging you for that trip either."

A smile formed on the gamekeeper's face. "Mrs McMurdo will be pleased wee me, seeing as my nephew's in demand. I'll even try Jock on the rig. Discuss this space camp wee him. If I'm lucky, I'll be first in line for the phone box."

"You're a star, Mr Keeper, but use this. It's quicker." NASA's social media guru handed him her cell.

The keeper laughed heartily for the first time, returning it to the American. "Aye, you can forget your fancy tech this far north, lassie. Nay signal. Even NASA has to rely on the red phone booth in Finkle."

48 Finkle

At the zenith of their power,
the Vikings left untouched only what they did not want.
Ved toppen av deira makt,
Vikingane let være urøyrd berre det dei ikkje ville ha.
Orcadian Sagas

The engine cut and three doors burst open.

"We're here then?" Pearl asked, over the clucking.

"Nay chivalry in this village," Mrs Mack grumbled, her parcels, the visitor, and the Landrover all abruptly abandoned. The keeper raced Auld Hamish and Farmer Dod, pulled by Jess on the short dash to the *Varrich Arms*.

A tower of lobster creels blocked Pearl's exit, forcing her to edge along the narrow strip of quayside, balancing with Mrs Mack's parcels. She was standing on a cobbled sloop that slipped into the water and her eyes were drawn to the fiery horizon.

The shopkeeper pointed at the seaweed next to Pearl's feet. "Careful, this place is beautiful but dangerous. Same can't be said about the locals." She grumbled and walked towards the whitewashed *Varrich Arms Hotel* and waited.

As the sun prepared to set, its last rays transformed the sheltered water into a shimmering blanket, casting long shadows over the ancient harbor wall. "Feels like I'm a million miles from NASA's problems already."

But she wasn't. All three candidates had to be delivered to Houston within forty-eight hours to avoid mission failure and the collapse of NASA as they knew it.

The coastal chorus was in full song: roosting seagulls, lapping waves, and the rhythmic chime of sailboat spinnakers clanking on masts that peeked above the boatyard wall.

"What does that mean?" Pearl pointed at the inscription in stone on the seawall. "Is that Gallic, or Scots tongue?"

"*Båtlaus mann er bunden til land.* Boatless man is tied to the land," Mrs Mack replied, opening the oak-paneled door to the pub. "It's Norwegian. Viking. You'll see."

Pearl selfied against the backdrop of the blue and green lobster boats rocking at anchor. When she looked up at the inn's hatched windows, bearded faces with pipes and tankards retreated.

The packed public bar fell silent as she made her entrance, amplifying the crackle of the log fire.

"She's wee me, and dinna be offering to help now," Mrs Mack announced from behind Pearl, balancing a tower of parcels, ignoring the two lobstermen rising slowly from the window seat. "What are you all gecking at anyway? Fine impression you're giving the lassie," she hurled at the patrons, barging past young Hamish the ferryman who was leaning against the bar.

Awkward conversations broke out like campfires across the room, its walls decorated with a thousand seafarers.

"And stop talking Gallic," Mrs. Mack turned the color of port. "Half of yooz cannae even speak it," she accused, vanishing into the kitchen in search of her sister, the bar returning to a frenzy of dominos, laughter, and clinking glass.

The trap door sprang open to reveal Aunty Bessie shouldering a barrel. The most popular, hardworking, and direct person in Finkle, she rolled the empty keg over the granite flagstones towards the door. "So sorry to have kept you waiting, my dear. We've been expecting you though. Your bed's all made up in the Mackie Tartan suite, overlooking our lovely wee harbor. Tea will be at seven pm after I've thrown this lot *oot, hame* to their pining wives." Bessie kicked the hatch closed as young Hamish fixed his fisherman's cap.

"Friends call me the ferryman."

"Or pensioner," shouted Bessie from the kitchen.

He ignored her and extended his anchor-tattooed hand. "Dod says you work for FIFA. Nae much of a football fan myself."

"NASA! You deaf old git," corrected the voice from the kitchen. "The space folk. You've nae even had your first dram and your jibbering."

"NASA, that's what I said, woman!" He shouted at the kitchen. "Argh, my hearing's not what it used to be. Well, I wish you every success while you're here, lassie. Anything the *Sea Nymph* or I can do, just you ask. The keeper says you're needing to speak to his nephew?" Do you ken he's a Martian?"

Pearl looked at young Hamish sympathetically, guessing his age to be around seventy.

"Vegan!" interrupted the kitchen again. "Scott's a bleeding Vegan, nae a Martian, ya dafty. Away hame and feed your dog afore ya lose your mind completely."

"You see that cursed causeway oot there, Pearl? A thousand years ago, the Vikings sailed a full mile past it and built a fortress at the head of the sea loch. Varrich castle."

"Bruich castle," corrected Mrs Mack from the kitchen.

"Varrich, Bruich, all the same thing," The ferryman's voice dropped to a whisper. "Ruled Scotland for three hundred years from those very ramparts, they did. *Leaving untouched only what they did not want.*"

"*Vikingane let være urøyrd berre det dei ikkje ville ha,*" Mrs Mack repeated the phrase in Norwegian from the kitchen, mischievously.

"Away hame with your stories, Ferryman," Bessie scoffed. "And you should know better Mrs Mack. Winding him up like that."

"Nay stories, Bessie—fact. Documented in the *Orcadian Sagas*, so they are."

The Ferryman held up his empty glass, preparing for a toast. "Most of us in these parts are more Viking than Highlander."

"Speak for yourself, Ferryman," blasted one of the lobstermen from the window seat. "Those sagas, tales of old, best be left alone. Dark times for Alba, Scottish history."

"Aye, myth and dark legend," remarked the other, his brother.

"Dark times indeed," repeated the first lobsterman. "According to the writings, back in those days, you were either a crofter wee a boat, or a fisherman wee a croft. Until they came."

Pearl looked to the ferryman.

"The Vikings," his voice barely audible.

"You'll be shouting Finkle's motto next," Bessie winced.

"The ground will shake and tyrants tremble," young Hamish yelled, clambering onto his barstool, wavering.

"When free men take up the sword!" Rejoiced the bar in concert.

The ferryman winked at Pearl and doffed his cap. "You'll see what I mean at Hogmanay."

"New year," Bessie interpreted, noting the confused look on Pearl's face. "Aye, well, our bonny American guest is only staying for one night, and if you ask me, the Norsemen overstayed their welcome by three hundred years. Like yourself, Ferryman. If you continue to bore my guests with our Viking history, I'll boot you oot. Just like our ancestors did to the Vikings a thousand years ago."

Hamish smiled. "Aye well, when Finkle gets in your blood, you dinnae want to leave. Why would anyone?"

49 Talmine

"Skol!" The ferryman toasted his brother in Norwegian, having secured his drink at happy hour prices.

"Slainte!" Cheers, the taximan replied the Highland way, holding his glass aloft.

Half the village was proud of their Norwegian heritage, half suspicious. Many nights had been spent debating how they'd react if the Norsemen invaded again.

"You promised!" Pearl flashed her Hollywood smile to the taximan holding court at the fireplace. He placed his untouched dram on the hearth and motioned for her to follow, saluting the ferryman as they snuck out the tradesman's exit.

"Hey min, what aboot your round. Ya tight auld git," his brother shouted after him.

"Talmine bay, you say," Hamish confirmed, reversing along the knife-edge quayside. "This time of day? Must be important."

"The future of human space flight depends on it," Pearl confirmed without hesitation. The rest of the five minute journey passed in unusual silence for the chatty man.

The Landrover crunched to a halt on the beach. Hamish kept its engine running as he glanced back over the water to the *Varrich Arms*. Pearl left the door wide open as she stepped down onto the sparkling shingle and walked towards the long white sands, spellbound.

Auld Hamish rolled down the window, shifted into reverse, and paused to let the American embrace the view as she approached the surf. "Hasn't changed since I was a lad. It'll be dark soon, so, if he's nae on the islet, look out for Badger's lights."

"I thought Badger was a dog?"

"Watch that estuary. She runs backward this time of day," he warned the city girl, spinning all four wheels in the direction of Finkle.

Pearl gazed at the pink horizon, the sea twinkling in the last light. Her thoughts were lost in the ebb and flow of the breaking waves, her mission fading blissfully with the daylight.

The sound of the taximan's horn outside the *Varrich Arms* drew her attention back across the estuary, as he returned to his waiting dram, and she took her second selfie against Finkle's huddle of colorful stone buildings in the distance.

Pearl followed the fresh animal tracks in the sand, disturbing a flock of seagulls feeding on the narrowing sandbar connecting Talmine beach to the largest islet. Avoiding the gull's fishy pickings, she knelt to inspect the trail. By the direction of the cloven hoof prints, the animals were headed back to the beach. Deducing Scott must be at the Mellness spaceport already, she rose and stumbled into the shallows. Just as she took a step in the freezing water, an eagle swooped overhead, escaping with a gull's pickings in its talons. Pearl cursed the scavenger as the mud sucked her down and her feet set like concrete. Unable to move her legs, she half fell and then righted herself. She was rapidly knee-deep in the icy shallows and reached for her cell as the seabirds mocked from above. "911 emergency," before correcting herself. "999 coastguard,", remembering the UK's emergency service number. The screen flashed *No Signal*.

Pearl strobed her cell's flashlight hoping someone—anyone—would see. Within minutes the icy water gripped her by the waist and surf broke over her back. The picturesque sky disappeared and was replaced by angry black clouds, as the darkness rolled in with the riptide.

50 Mellness

The five foot high, three mile long, chainmail fence that surrounded the Mellness spaceport wasn't working. The evidence was rampaging around the launch pad.

Antler clashed with antler as the sparring intensified. The stags reclaimed their territory while the hinds congregated around the launch tower, more interested in the shelter and good grazing at its base than the show.

The keeper had warned them and the elders had listened, but the councilors ignored the advice—Lowland thinking in the Highlands doesn't work.

It was agreed at the last clan gathering that Inverness would supply the fence and the keeper would manage site security. The council didn't understand the ways of the land though, nor did they have the first clue about the space business.

"Naebody does." The keeper's wisdom still echoed around Finkle's Village Hall.

Mrs Mack minuted the action: Complain to the clan's chieftain when he returned from the rigs.

The keeper had always been there for Scott, no matter what, who, or why. The same could not be said for his father, Jock McMurdo, the chieftain.

The boy relished the responsibility delegated by his uncle and this was one battle he wasn't going to lose. Having repaired the fence, he needed to free the deer before they did any more damage to themselves or the launch site.

Scott worked faster than the approaching storm, placing *Chirp* a quarter mile from the perimeter fence at the base of Eagle Tree, its bark scarred by generations of stags marking their territory, scratching velvet from itching antlers.

Scott dug the device into the base of the tree and set the timer as its winged residents divebombed protectively overhead. The attack continued as he raced back to Badger—beaks shrieking, talons snapping, the eagles escaping with his baseball cap. The retreat to the launchpad gates was a relief as he bounced his trusty Landrover over the grouse moor in slow motion.

Scott ditched Badger as his smartwatch sounded early, and made the final ten meter dash through the heather on foot, colliding with the gates as they refused to open. *Chirp* was already barking the stag's mating call and he cursed as the hooves tore towards him, his frozen fingers struggling with the combination lock.

"Wrong!" He shouted, forgetting the code, trying birthday after birthday.

The call of the annual rut boomed for a second time that season, luring the herd in a frenzy of mating excitement.

"1969. Jock's Birthday," he muttered under his breath. "Of all the—" Scott rolled under Badger as the gates sprang open, unleashing the rampant beasts on the moor. He smiled as the confused hinds disappeared into the hollows of the glen and the duped stags stampeded towards Eagle Tree.

His chore completed and his heart pounding, he looked out over the rugged landscape, watching the patches of brilliant purple and brown heather fade with the light. His thoughts returned to Runa and her hostage.

51 Badger

The rumble of thunder reminded Scott of his promise to get farmer Dod home before the storm hit. The quickest route to the *Varrich Arms* was to skirt Talmine beach, risk the backside of the causeway, and take the fields to Finkle Farm, as long as he wasn't spotted by McFearson, the local and only police constable.

Every rise and fall in the dunes was familiar to the pair—driver and vehicle—as they glided their way towards the shoreline overlooking Finkle.

Scott peered through the twilight, slowing at the top of the rise, spying something unusual in the estuary. A boat had broken free from its mooring. Stranded on the sandbar where he'd been only an hour earlier, it strobed a blue light. "McFearson," Scott said to Badger, talking to the Landrover like an old friend.

Finkle's police constable was either snooping on the outsider's spaceport or a member of the McMurdo clan. That was his day job and Scott had to deal with it. McFearson craved the chieftain's position held by Jock, Scott's father, and he resented the clan leader's absence. His vendetta against all who held the name McMurdo was as relentless as it was legendary.

"He'll only catch us in Finkle. Might earn us some brownie points if we help him," Scott murmured to Badger.

Flicking on the Landrover's powerful spotlights. He couldn't believe what he saw. A green jacket waved frantically, submerged to the shoulders on what had been the sandbar. Someone was stuck fast in the mud.

"Here goes nothing," Scott shouted as he veered toward the shoreline, flashing SOS with his headlamps and surfing four tons of steel down the dunes. He prayed the lifeboat crew was watching from Finkle as he rammed Badger onto the shingle just feet from the breaking waves. He made one last possibly futile blast of Morse: three-short flashes, three-long, three-short.

He slammed Badger's fender-mounted winch into neutral and spooled out the entire length of its nylon line. Winding hand over elbow, he placed the coil on the ground as the waves whipped at his heels. Scott jumped onto the Defender's hood and grabbed the snorkel with both hands. "Sorry buddy, needs must," he apologized, ripping off the air intake tube, snatching a marine flare from the cab, and duct-taping the winch line to its shaft. "One rocket. One chance to get this right."

He pointed the makeshift bazooka high and downstream of the casualty, favoring the racing tide over the raging wind, and pulled the ripcord, launching the missile.

Scott grimaced at the whoosh, his cheek scorched, as his hands felt the rope spool wildly through the snorkel. The coil at his feet lashed like a tornado of angry snakes, and the snap-crack suggested rocket and line had parted company. The explosion against the council hall confirmed the missile had cleared the estuary. The line recoiled, left floating in the water twenty feet from the victim's grasp.

Scott followed the lifeline with Badger's fox lamp, scouring the December sea, praying it would drift in the right direction.

He cupped his hands. "Swim to the rope. Tie it around you!"

Pearl lowered her arms into the icy water. With every ounce of remaining strength, she stretched towards the line. The punishing tide slapped her in the face, as her feet sank deeper in the sludge, hands numb to the bone. Her unfeeling fingertips touched the rope but weren't capable of grasping. Pearl lashed out against the cruel black water submerged and disoriented. Her arm hooked the line and her survival instinct took control.

Scott raced to Badger's winch and began reeling in slowly, fretting as the line tightened against the human cargo trapped in the mud. "Nothing for it," he yelled to no one, as he wound the drum, watching the figure launch like a jumping salmon. The line cat-balled, jamming the winch.

He hauled harder than a lobsterman, hand over hand, dragging the dead weight to shore. He scanned the shallows. "I'm coming in!" he yelled, as he waded through the crashing surf towards the prone figure, grabbing the green jacket, staring in disbelief at the shivering girl's wide smile.

Scott pointed at her bare feet, then the Landrover, finding the words. "Hurry, unless you want to kill both of us," he guided her towards the cab and gestured towards the assortment of oily coveralls, fisherman's jumpers, farmer's Jackets. "Take your pick. It's these or hypothermia."

Scott cranked up the Landrover's heater, shuddering the vehicle into reverse and out of the surf, crunching over the driftwood. "You owe me for a snorkel," he said to the bedraggled face in the rearview mirror.

In the five minutes it took to reach the causeway, Scott listened, Badger whined, and Pearl thawed and talked. By the time they reached the *Varrich Arms*, she was still briefing him, and he could see his opportunity.

There was no way his father would ignore him now.

"Thanks," Pearl said as they arrived on the quayside. "Not a single question?"

"Only one."

"Shoot."

"Does that jacket come in red?" Scott made the NASA polar connection.

The rest of his questions about Runa's extraction would have to wait if he stood any chance of keeping his promise to Farmer Dod.

Two Landrovers blocked the quayside, one illegally. Pearl puzzled at what the adolescent had asked as she approached the oak door flapping in the wind. The inn fell silent for the second time that evening as the mud-covered girl presented herself in farmer's overalls, a fisherman's jumper, and gamekeeper's boots, her eyes wide.

The lobstermen stood abruptly. The ferryman nodded approvingly. "Welcome to Finkle, lassie. You're one of us now!" The bar returned to its version of normal.

52 Eagle Tree

"Finkle, we have a problem," the keeper said.

The blanket dropped from Pearl's shoulders as she lowered the steaming mug of coffee and broke from the huddle around the roaring fire.

"The chieftain does nae like it," the keeper continued. The group shuffled to make space around the hearth for him.

"Mostly the idea of the boy going abroad wee strangers."

"I'm right here!" Scott complained.

"Aye, and you're fourteen years old!" Mrs Mack shouted from the kitchen.

"No doubt it'll get you noticed by your absent father," Bessy said, pushing her way to the bar with half a dozen empty tankards.

"If I do this, I do it for Finkle," Scott said fiercely. "And I will be doing it."

"I know you will, love," Bessy replied.

"Not for Groundswell?" asked Dod.

"Aye, them too, but Finkle needs all the help it can get, right?" Scott looked to NASA's intern.

"I get it," Pearl replied, winking at the boy. "The thing is, Scott won't be alone, I'll be chaperoning."

Bessy rescued Pearl from the silence that followed. "Somebody ging oot and close the shutters afore the windows blow in," she yelled at the unmoving bar.

Pearl read their faces, knowing it was make or break, and played her bluff. "Runa Erikson and Chase Hudson—Scott's best friends—are en route to Houston as we speak." Her mission confidence wavered.

"I'm still here," Scott protested again at the sound of their names. "Let's go," he motioned toward the exit. Jess barked excitedly, clenching her lead between her teeth.

"Not so fast," Farmer Dod cautioned. "I dinnae mean to sound harsh like, but you can see it from Jock's point of view. NASA turns up unannounced, wee your fantastic story, and Scott's expected to disappear off with you into space, wee two pals he's never met?"

"I'm in," Scott repeated.

Pearl remained silent and patted Jess on the head.

"I'm just saying," Dod grumbled, staring into the hissing flames as the rain blew down the chimney. Jess licked Pearl's hand lavishly, her tail wagging. "Aye well, she's a good judge of character that *yin*. So, we'll hear you out."

The inn fell unusually silent.

"Any of you are welcome to accompany Scott to Houston," Pearl replied. "NASA's got a plane unloading launch equipment in Inverness right now. It leaves tomorrow at 1200 hours."

The keeper stood looking as excited as a child at Christmas. "Well, I've always wanted to see America."

"Ya ken, the Vikings found it first—America!" The Ferryman shouted from the bar.

"Away with your havering nonsense," Bessie heckled.

"Eric the Red. Five hundred years afore the boy Columbus. It's all in the book," defended the Ferryman.

"Nay evidence," shouted the lobsterman.

"You and your dusty books. He's aff again aboot the *Orcadian Sagas*," complained the lobsterman's brother, returning to his tankard.

The keeper's shoulders dropped. "But I've got responsibilities. Deer, pheasants, ferrets, and Mrs McMurdo. So, I cannae just take off," he pointed at Farmer Dod and Auld Hamish. "And neither of them hay a passport."

Dod shrugged, prodding his old friend. "Glad to see you still know how to take a nap, Hamish. Wake up, man."

Pearl glanced at Scott, her eyes prompting him to speak.

"It's only for a week or so," Scott pleaded. "Back in time for Christmas. I'm almost thirteen. You forget when I traveled to Norway on my own to meet my dad between crew changes." Scott gave his uncle a telling look. "I was stuck in Stavanger for three days at the B&B he arranged. Boker og Borst—booze and books. Mind you, they made a nice Lava latte for kids. He was snowed in at Trondheim five hundred miles away, or so he claimed. Remind him of that!"

Pearl seized on her opportunity. "If we can convince Jock to let Scott attend even the interview, NASA will be eternally grateful. We can supercharge the spaceport petition. Heck, half the launch gear's already in Inverness. Most of the equipment for the cube satellite launches is too wide for the local roads. So, it'll have to arrive by either heavy-lift chopper, or by ship. Way too big for Finkle's harbor. Young Hamish and his Sea Nymph will be in demand."

The Ferryman moved through the bar, hearing his name. Arm resting on his brother's shoulder, he leaned towards the fire as Pearl padded her offer. "Seriously, guys, there'll be a thriving, lucrative industry here, generating skilled jobs in no time."

An awed silence spread across the inn. Pearl braced herself for the riptide of counteroffers.

"Harbor repairs," shouted the lobstermen from the window seat.

Auld Hamish opened his right eye, a sly look transforming his face. "A mobile phone mast for the village and free broadband for the community—that might help convince the chieftain."

Dod nodded, looking to the keeper. "Aye, the school could do with a wee lick of paint and some new playground equipment."

"Heck, we'll even throw in a trip to Space City for every kid in the village," Pearl replied, drawing on her reserves. "Just as long as Scott makes that flight tomorrow."

"If adults go too, I'll call Jock back right now," the keeper said, making for the exit.

"Wait!" Scott shouted at his uncle as he reached the front door. "Tell him NASA will move Eagle Tree out of harm's way." He looked to Pearl for approval, and she nodded.

The lobstermen rejoiced, raising Scott triumphantly on their shoulders as Big Angus shot out the door.

Minutes later, the keeper returned coated in sweat, his voice agitated. "Finkle, we hay another problem."

"Thought you'd gone ta America withoot the lad?" The voices echoed around the fireplace.

"Well, I telt the queue ootside it was a matter of national importance. We need another phone box. NASA, add that to your list!"

Blue flashing lights filled the windows.

"And I telt yooz to close those shutters," Bessie hollered from behind the bar.

A third Landrover screeched to a halt outside the inn, barricading the quayside.

53 Bagpipes

From the fury of the Northmen deliver us, O Lord.
Frels oss Herre, frå nordmennene sitt raseri.
Orcadian Sagas

"What have you done now, loon?" Farmer Dod turned to Scott in alarm. "Quick, oot the back door, and dinnae touch Badger."

The front door sprang open to reveal Finkle's police constable, backed up by a smirking, scrawny kid a few years older than Scott.

"McMurdo," the officer yelled. "Who was driving the illegal Landrover ootside?"

Every hand in the bar rose.

"Going to be like that is it?" The constable took a deep breath. "Somebody fired a rocket from Talmine at the council hall."

"Hopefully, it burnt to the groond," the ferryman scoffed, foaming his beer as he laughed. "Wee the useless lot that runs it." He wiped the froth from his beard at the sound of jeering from the bar.

"Well, naebody's leaving till I find oot who it was." McFearson approached the Ferryman, his voice vengeful. "And I'm starting wee Scott McMurdo. Where's he hiding?" He pushed through the crowded bar, heading for the keeper's usual spot.

Bessie stopped collecting glasses and squared up to the constable, blocking his path. "Ye cannae just burst in here making unfounded accusations. The culprit's surely your boy, Weasel." She pointed at the skinny teenager cowering behind McFearson. "He's been envious of Scott for years, that one. Likely pinched the lobsterman's flares again. Away oot man, afore I bar you for good. Scott's nae guilty."

"I'll be asking fae the last time," McFearson continued undeterred, turning full circle. "Afore I ticket every car ootside."

"There are only three, and one of them's yours, ya wazzak," somebody heckled.

The furious constable reached for his book, eyeing the taximan.

The Ferryman grabbed the bagpipes hanging on the wall. *"Frels oss Herre, frå nordmennene sitt raseri."* From the fury of the northmen deliver us, O Lord, he hollered, quoting from the plaque above the bar. He squeezed the pipes with his elbow, bringing them to life with a deep breath. The inn descended into chaos and the sound of *Scotland the Brave*. The whooping and twirling of wild highland dance sent glasses sloshing and patrons spinning, buying time for NASA's escape.

McFearson and Weasel fought through the Celtic revelers toward the fireplace, reaching the crescent bench and finding it empty, three half-full glasses, and two steaming mugs left suspiciously on the floor. The constable searched, yelling with frustration as the plump lobstermen closed in on his son, blocking his path, demanding their flares.

McFearson pounded on the bolted back door, cursed, turned, and bumped into Weasel edging backward. He snatched the boy from the clutches of one lobsterman, only to be trapped by the other bolting the front door, tossing the keys to Bessy.

"Dinnae, you dare!" the policeman warned as the ferryman paused only to mop his brow.

"Lock in!" The lobstermen hollered over the drone of the pipes.

Two Landrovers reversed along the jetty in darkness, away from the strobing blue lights. Farmer Dod and the keeper were in Badger, followed by Pearl at the wheel of the taxi, with Auld Hamish and Scott riding shotgun on its bench. Badger crunched to a halt on the barnacle-covered sloop. Dod winced at the waves licking the tailgate as the keeper motioned for Pearl to pass him on the narrow, cobbled street. "Take the back roads to Inverness," he yelled. "Auld Hamish'll keep you right. We'll block the law in wee all four tons of this. We'll gee you a thirty minute head start. There's only one road out of Finkle. McFearson does nae ken where you're going, so you'll be fine. Drive carefully and watch oot for the big reds on the roads this time of night. Best o' luck, lad. I never doubted you."

"I'll make you proud. You'll see," Scott shouted excitedly.

"I already am. More than you'll ever know," the keeper replied with a lump in his throat. "Off you go and save the world afore McFearson leaves the party."

Their work done for the night, the Highlanders blended into the hillside, leaving Scott staring back in the direction of the blue lights at the phone box. "I need to phone Runa."

"Later," Pearl crunched the gears. "We have to make Inverness by daybreak."

"Dinnae worry lad," the taximan said, yawning. "The next phone box is in Wick, only two hours away.

54 Ellington

Where wolves' ears are, wolves' teeth are near.
Er du nær ulvens øyrer så pass deg for tennene.

"*Jeg advarte deg*! I warned you," Runa Erikson said, finding herself trapped on NASA One while the ground crew feigned problems with its landing gear. She pushed passed Fox Washington to listen to the radio chatter about a missing aircraft. This doesn't feel right, she thought as she peered out the cockpit window to the silver whale-like plane dwarfing them on the runway, its propellers still turning, its fuselage graffitied with insults about NASA. "The deal's off," she said watching the man approaching NASA One crouch on the runway.

"Coming in hot!" The radio in the cockpit barked.

The 1998 Sikorsky Superhawk swooped over NASA's Ellington Air force Base, trailing smoke, its sole pilot as desperate as his passengers to set down after a thousand bone-shaking miles. He nursed the overheating chopper as it hovered on fumes, homing in on a figure waving lights next to the blackened fuselage of NASA One. The veteran wished he had a horn as he bore down on the ground crew, attempting a wheels-up landing.

Runa studied the man on the tarmac as he returned to his feet. He leaned into the helicopter's storm, gripping the peak of his NASA cap, protecting files under his arm. He waited until the blades drooped before advancing. His path blocked by the fire crew as they raced to dowse the smoke billowing from its undercarriage.

The subject of an international incident, NASA One had been forced to respect radio silence since their escape from Svalbard. Candidate Viking had had enough. She knew NASA was stalling by the look on Fox's face. Not that she needed any proof. The space agency had disguised its tracks from the start. They'd highjacked the world's most popular game, bribed three communities, and lured three kids to this destination. But where were her friends? And why was she being held captive?

As the sun rose to reveal the bizarre beauty pageant of smoking, sparking, graffitied aircraft, her mind was set. *Han viser aldri tennene som ikkje kan bite.* If you cannot bite, never show your teeth. Runa Erikson had had enough.

The explosion forced everyone on the tarmac to their knees.

Huck Chambers placed his palms on the tarmac like a sprinter in the blocks, pressing down on the papers as the Lear jet's door detonated open, and he rolled back to dodge the evacuation chute as it inflated.

"For Odin sin kjærleik," Runa muttered to herself. For the love of Odin. They're not here, she fretted, standing at the hatch, wrapped in her Arctic down jacket and swinging the emergency release.

Chambers brushed himself down and offered an awkward salute. "Welcome to Houston."

Runa slid down the chute cross-legged, landing on the runway and staring at her captor.

"Where's my team? Chase Hudson, Scott McMurdo?" she demanded.

Chambers studied the teenager.

Candidate One, codenamed Viking. The girl's entrance matched her online persona: tough and competent. The future of NASA's human space flight program depended on her. She just didn't know it yet.

"My name is Huck Chambers, I run NASA's Mission-X selection program."

"I know. I read your dossier on the plane. Twice." Runa eyed him with suspicion. "This is going to be a short trip if I have to ask where my team is again."

Huck nodded, encouraging her to approach the fiasco developing around the chopper.

The helicopter pilot exited first, wading into the foam, and surveyed the damage to his pride and joy. Chase Hudson, Candidate Two, staggered out next, leaving a second passenger wrestling with his four-point seat harness in the cabin.

"Quite the entrance you just made," Runa extended her hand, her face hinted at a smile.

"Dark departure, Dude," Chase replied, unsure if he should hug or fist bump with this friend he'd never met. He nodded towards their aircraft. "When do we talk about what just happened?"

"Later," Runa gestured cautiously towards Huck Chambers, pleating her hair against the wind from the chopper's idling blades. She pointed at the trapped figure in the smoldering helicopter. "Who's your passenger?"

"I'll explain if you do?" Chase countered, pointing at Fox Washington in his red jacket as he stood in the hole of the fuselage. Their sarcasm was interrupted by a shout.

"Runa! Chase!" Candidate Three codenamed Highlander. Scott McMurdo escaped from the enormous alien looking craft parked next to them. The boy hung out the fuselage door as the mobile steps approached. He took them five at a time and tackled his friends to the ground. "NASA's delivered this time.".

Chambers watched the spontaneous jumping huddle of teenagers through the commotion on the airfield and returned the papers to his inside pocket. Phase one of Mission-X neared completion, meaning phase two loomed.

Runa cautioned her friends, looking at the man from NASA in the shadows. *"Er du nær ulvens øyrer så pass deg for tennene.* Where wolves' ears are, wolves' teeth are near."

55 Triple-A

Repay treachery with lies
Møt foræderi med foræderi og løgn med løgn

The early morning rays baked the tarmac, engulfing the candidates in a ghostly mist.

Runa felt it first. The ridiculousness of their situation, the rise of Groundswell, Season 9, and their impossible journey to infamy.

They looked at each other. Their virtual connection had transformed into a physical bond.

Runa clasped her talisman and whispered the Viking wisdom, *"Søk noko, risiker alt."* Seek something, risk everything. Their new play. Knowing this day marked the end of their childhood, she offered her friends a reassuring look and Groundswell's catchphrase. "Gaming is Good."

They heard a staged cough from behind and turned towards Huck Chambers.

"Who's the guy?" Scott whispered. "Trouble?"

"Maybe," Runa replied. "But for now, he's the only thing standing between us and our dream for Groundswell."

Huck beckoned the teenagers to follow him. Runa hesitated, studying NASA's interns as they converged.

The girl that exited Scott's plane waved in a familiar way to Fox from the top step. She was dressed in oily overalls, farmer's boots, and a herring bone jumper tied around her waist. She paused halfway down, surprised by his appearance. A three-day beard covered his chiseled jaw, and he had darkened circles for eyes, his red jacket in tatters. Runa re-tied her snowboots as she listened to the exchange.

"What happened?" the girl asked in alarm. "Click and collect, you said?"

Fox cracked a smile. "Didn't go quite to plan." He nodded towards Runa, then the paint-splattered Guppy. "Least the asset's on the ground. Don't know what's worse, your outfit, or the paint job? Experience a little mission-creep yourself?"

"As you say, brother, the candidate's on location," she replied, pointing at Scott as the Asian intern arrived.

"My guy's over there, that's all I've got to say." Sing pointed to Chase.

Runa ran protectively to her friends as the sound wave struck.

Three Apache AH-64 attack helicopters flew in low and fast in tight formation, their updraft buffeting even the massive transport plane.

The aircraft hovered threateningly over the tarmac, boasting army, air force, and navy insignia. Huck rushed through the retreating fire crew, corralling his teams from the storm of noise towards the safety of the hanger. The teenagers refused to comply.

Runa stood her ground, facing off the monstrous machines, shielding her friends from the fearful wind as the Apaches opened their cargo doors in unison.

The central gunship raised its chin before ejecting a hard-looking man in his fifties who landed like a cat. Dressed in air force fatigues, he scanned the site.

Three balaclava-clad figures followed him out onto the tarmac, one from each of the aircraft. They gathered around the cat man before breaking out and charging towards the trio.

"Final fight!" Somebody yelled.

Runa, Scott, and Chase formed a defensive perimeter, bracing themselves with nothing more than clenched fists and steely looks.

A Humvee blocked the attackers' path, tires screeching.

"Møt foræderi med foræderi og løgn med løgn!" Repay treachery with lies, Runa cursed, losing line of sight as the Humvee obscured the squad. This was all NASA's doing. They had been betrayed again. Runa was as convinced of this as she was of her Viking DNA.

The Humvee revved its powerful engine. All armor and aerials, its rear doors opened beckoning the black-clad squad. They entered as one, and the last figure turned, revealing her identity, a girl no older than Runa.

A billion dollars of military machine made its thunderous retreat, leaving Groundswell, their dreams, and their chances of selection in its wake.

"You just met the Triple-A Team," Huck Chambers said, tapping Runa from behind. "Your competition."

"Game on!" The steel in her voice cut through the din of the rotors.

Epilogue

NASA INTERNAL COMMUNICATION: EYES ONLY.

RE: Title: Accelerated Evolution "Project Bones"

Date: Fri 6th December

Launch Date: T-minus six months

To: "Mission-X"

From: Building 9

Sender: Professor Cornelius Allbright

Hijacking the world's most popular game to identify our candidates, while controversial, has proved successful. Delivering our team of tough, competent, teenagers in time for bio-screening has not been without consequences. Nor will their path to low Earth orbit be without danger, as space travel is neither safe nor easy.

It is no secret that Director One craves the crown of overlord. He longs to serve as head of the newly formed US Space Force at the pleasure of the president. The new organization seeks the militarization of space, and hostile flags of conquest on the Moon, Mars, and beyond.

Project Bones will be our savior. Candidates Viking, Highlander, and Mariner are already racing against their biological clocks, forcing us to combine years of training into months. By launching these unique adolescents into space, we will see how gravity cheats Mother Nature and watch her change our candidates' DNA forever. The zero-G experiment, Accelerated Evolution, will deliver the perfect biological astronaut capable of withstanding the rigors of deep space, proving human interstellar travel is neither lethal nor unethical. NASA's future as a peaceful pioneer of space exploration must prevail for generations to come.

As you know, there are forces within NASA already working against us, willing our demise and lusting after our twenty billion dollar budget. I implore you to trust only NINE.

Your mission is threefold;

1. Ensure our candidates are fit to fly.

2. Deliver them safely into orbit.

3. Deliberately put them in harm's way.

End of Message.

Professor Cornelius Allbright

Chief Scientist NASA

Acknowledgments

Editor: Sue Fitzmaurice, Rebel Magic Books

Nordic Translation: Helge Rutledal

Cover Artist: Dave at JD&J Design

Kjell Henriksen Observatory KHO Head Engineer: Mikko Syrjäsuo,

NASA's NBL diver and Zero G instructor (Retired): Hyang Llloyd

NASA's Chief of Research Assurance: Charles W. Lloyd

Scottish NASA Society: Colin Black.

Beta readers: Jacob Tom, Nina Bilak

Read the next in the series: subscribe at groundswellsagas.com

About the Author

Born in Scotland, hardened by Norway. DJ turned diver turned author, Garrad launches the Groundswell Sagas.

**REBEL
MAGIC
BOOKS**

www.rebelmagicbooks.com

Printed in Great Britain
by Amazon